P9-CAA-076

For Linda—

Going Away Shoes

stories

Jill McCorkle

With best wishes!
Jill McCorkle

a shannon ravenel book

ALGONQUIN BOOKS OF CHAPEL HILL 2009

10/02/09

IR
A SHANNON RAVENEL BOOK

Published by
ALGONQUIN BOOKS OF CHAPEL HILL
Post Office Box 2225
Chapel Hill, North Carolina 27515-2225

a division of
WORKMAN PUBLISHING
225 Varick Street
New York, New York 10014

© 2009 by Jill McCorkle.
All rights reserved.
Printed in the United States of America.
Published simultaneously in Canada by Thomas Allen & Son Limited.
Hand lettering by Lisa Fyfe

Stories originally appeared, sometimes in different form, in the following periodicals and collections, to whose editors grateful acknowledgment is made: "Going Away Shoes" in *Blackbird*, "Surrender" in *The Oxford American*, "Midnight Clear" in *The Southern Review*, "Another Dimension" and "Magic Words" in *Narrative*, "Happy Accidents" in *Agni*, "View-Master" in *The Washington Post Magazine*, "Intervention" in *Ploughshares*, *Best American Short Stories*, and *New Stories from the South*, "Me and Big Foot" and "Driving to the Moon" in *The American Scholar*, and "PS" in *The Atlantic*.

This is a work of fiction. While, as in all fiction, the literary perceptions and insights are based on experience, all names, characters, places, and incidents either are products of the author's imagination or are used fictitiously. No reference to any real person is intended or should be inferred.

LIBRARY OF CONGRESS CATALOGING-IN-PUBLICATION DATA
McCorkle, Jill, [date]
Going away shoes : stories / Jill McCorkle.—1st ed.
p. cm.
"A Shannon Ravenel book."
ISBN-13: 978-1-56512-632-9
I. Title.
PS3563.C3444G65 2009
813'.54—dc22 2009011706

10 9 8 7 6 5 4 3 2 1
First Edition

Going Away Shoes

Also by JILL McCORKLE

NOVELS

The Cheer Leader
July 7th
Tending to Virginia
Ferris Beach
Carolina Moon

STORIES

Crash Diet
Final Vinyl Days
Creatures of Habit

For Tom, with love

and as always, for Claudia and Rob

If the shoe doesn't fit, must we change the foot?

—GLORIA STEINEM

CONTENTS

Going Away Shoes

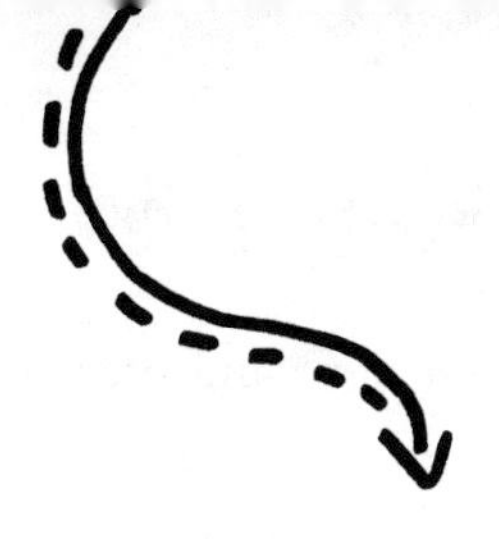

GOING AWAY SHOES

DEBBY TYLER IS A mythical stereotype, the oldest child who stays home to tend the sick and dying mother while her sisters marry and have prosperous lives elsewhere. They pity her, she can tell. They tell her stories of late-blooming love and how they want to send her on a cruise, something batted around every year before the holidays but has yet to materialize. "It could happen, Debby," they say. "Remember *The Love Boat*?"

Does she remember *The Love Boat*? Shit. She still watches *The Love Boat* on those afternoons when she needs sounds and distractions but is too tired to read. What do they think she can possibly do all day while emptying a bedpan and answering to nonsensical screams and requests and more recently just monitoring vital signs and preventing bedsores. She knows all the reruns, nature shows, game shows, and soaps. Though when all is said and done, the soaps are the best place to be—vapid and dramatic people and situations and thus familiar to what she has witnessed her whole life in this very house.

THE TYLER FAMILY myth is old, overused, and unoriginal and yet very much alive, as family myths are in so many households, feeding and thriving on the pretense that everyone is happy and A-OK, that in fact they are a unique family to be so happy and A-OK. And of course there are a few characters in the family. The lineage includes an Icarus type, brilliant but doomed Uncle Ted, who crashed his Cessna, killing himself and two women he'd met at a convention called BoyToysRUs while en route to another convention called Beat Me in St. Louis. And a Persephone, rescued by her mother from the underworld, in the form of Wanda, Debby's sister, who was shacked up with Paulie Long in a drug den, and their mother got all dressed up and drove down to Smyrna to get her. Wanda then had to go to rehab, which was referred to as "Wanda's much needed vacation from the stresses of young womanhood." The experience returned her rigid and righteous and ready to save any and all who were on a different path, a choice in Debby's opinion that was just as bad and *should* be illegal.

Debby's other sister, Carly, would be Narcissus. She always

has an eye in a mirror or window while watching herself conduct *The Carly Show*, which is all about Carly's face and body, what's new and changing. In fact, Carly, Wanda, and their mother all fit the Narcissus profile, whole lives jockeying for the hall mirror or those on the car visors. Even on Debby's graduation day, when she needed somebody to button that shitty white eyelet empire-waist dress she was made to wear, she could not get help because they were all involved in doing their own hair and hose and zippers as if *they* were the ones about to stand up as salutatorian and say the prayer. *God, don't let me turn into them*, she prayed in that moment, before really offering a more general prayer about healthy strong minds and those people who nurture them. She saw them there in the front row—her father dozing, mother turning to nod to those who wanted to tell her what a good job she had done with Debby, sisters looking around to see who might be looking at them and interested in asking them out.

"I still don't see why you left out the Lord," her mother said afterwards. "I had written it on your paper—'In Jesus name I pray.' Didn't you see where I wrote that?" Her mother went on to say how her dress was buttoned crooked, how on earth did that happen. She bet the people there on the stage—the principal and vice principal and that girl she should have beaten out for the better spot—noticed it, too.

Sometimes Debby felt like Prometheus. Just when she got her

liver healthy and plump again, the eagle descended to peck on it. The eagle with piercingly dramatic mascaraed eyes and talons done perfectly in Revlon's Rich Girl Red.

Dear God, next time I have a whole liver, please break the chains and let me catch a Greyhound the fuck out of here.

It's hard to watch a soap opera and *not* feel somewhat better about your own life—they have such *huge* problems and such *stupid* ways of expressing them. They say "I don't understand" every other line, which is a stall tactic used to carry things over to a commercial. It's like back before they had the shot clock in basketball and a team could just stand there dribbling and passing the time away. That's what she's doing there at her mother's bedside, dribbling and passing the time away.

The caretaker. She is *the caretaker.* They call her this with praise in their voices, usually after mentioning the phantom cruise, other times after reciting all the wonderful things they have recently accomplished, a recital that never allows them to look her in the eye. They look so little they didn't even notice she has recently highlighted her hair, that she is in great condition—better abs than either of them—thanks to *Sunrise Pilates* on the local channel.

And there's the real answer: they can't look and see her as a person with needs and desires the same as theirs. That would be way too difficult. There is clearly some shame, just not enough. They can rationalize that she gets to live for free because she is the one stationed in their mother's house. That's what the slave owners said, too. Good room and board. They have convinced themselves that were she not tending their mother, Debby would be all alone in some piece of crap house barely making ends meet. (She never came close to marriage, they often say.) They all know that the will provides for equal distribution of everything, including this house, and no one has ever suggested it should be otherwise. "If I have a dollar when I die," their mother has said since they were children, "then each of my girls will get thirty-three cents and we will give that final cent to the Lord."

"Wow," Debby said once, laughing, "the Lord won't know what to do with all that." She was still working full-time at the local paper then, covering social events and activities in town: engagement and retirement and silver wedding anniversary celebrations, ceremonies for Eagle Scouts and 4-H and the DAR. She was thorough without being boring; in fact people often told her they felt that they had been present at an event, she described it so well. She tried to make the most modest attempts (a church fellowship hall strewn with confetti, plates of pimento cheese–stuffed celery) seem elegantly simple, and those that were ostentatious (goody bags that equaled a week's salary for anyone earning minimum wage and floral displays trucked in from out of town) she let speak for themselves. It was a matter of selecting which facts to tell and which to leave out, obviously a tactic she had long observed and studied.

"I'll give the Lord 10 percent then, and maybe even more," her mother had said. Sometimes Debby's mother promised the Lord more when she didn't like the way Debby wrote something up. "Keep laughing at me, Debby Lynn Tyler, and the Lord will get every last goddamned cent."

Who knows where Debby would be or what she'd be doing had she not stepped in to help her mother. At the time it was no big deal; it would be a temporary bridge to a retirement village, where her mother might play cards and go on little group trips here and there, have her own little kitchenette. But almost as soon as Debby moved in, things went from bad to worse, and the place they had in mind was no longer an option. Their mother was in between a place where people are still living and thriving and one that is a kind of death row. So Debby is still here and she doesn't even know herself where she might be otherwise, and in recent years, she has stopped trying to imagine. Now she just freelances on occasion, sharing her expertise with younger reporters about how to describe a wedding without it sounding as awful as it was. "When the bride and groom read their own vows," she tells them, "don't even *try* to quote. And just tell the color of the bridesmaid dresses and that the bride wore white or ivory satin or silk or whatever. Simple is always best." It takes a while for them to learn, and some of them never do.

Our sister, the caretaker, bless her heart. Of course, if not for mother, she'd be all alone herself.

Caretaker sounds like Debby might be wandering some lovely rose garden, snipping away thorns and breathing in a heavy heavenly perfume. Instead she is changing Depends while trying not to humiliate this woman who gave her life just in case there is a moment of consciousness and clarity, the desire to make amends or to offer something that might resemble love. Those moments of consciousness do not come very often now and haven't for the last several weeks; the sound of the oxygen tank has taken over the house as if the very walls are expanding and contracting. If it were Debby lying there, she'd want to be unplugged. Nothing has been more horrible to watch than that woman on the news day in and day out, with her people arguing over her fate. If they'd cared at all, they'd have gotten those goddamned cameras out of the room and handled their business in a more dignified way. "Please Release Me, Let Me Go."—that was her mother's favorite song years ago, and whenever Debby thinks of it she pictures her mother at the kitchen sink, hair sprayed into a perfect little flip, apron cinched neatly around her wasp waist like all the mothers on the reruns—June Cleaver, Harriet Nelson, Margaret Anderson—only not like them at all.

Please release me, let me go.

Debby has contemplated writing a little note in what looks like her mother's handwriting saying as much: *I never want to be kept alive by unnatural means.* Debby could find the note in the bottom of one of her mother's purses and present it to her siblings the next time they pop in.

The purses—there are at least a hundred. Just two years ago when her mother was still mobile and before Debby moved in full-time, she would arrive to find her mother standing in the doorway waiting. If she came by from work at five in the afternoon, or if she ran outside to check the mail during a visit, when she reached the front door, her mother would be waiting there, purse clutched and ready to go. It reminded Debby of all those stories you hear about dogs, like Roosevelt's Fala, who never stopped waiting for his master's return. Or her mother's ancient chihuahua, Peppy, who never took his cloudy eyes off of his mistress even when he couldn't move from the tiny heating pad where he spent his last days. The vets would have you believe that dogs have no sense of time, that they don't sit for a week worried and wondering what you're doing on vacation. And isn't it easier to believe that? Debby had hoped that the same was true of her mother, her tiny bird shoulders sloping down, gnarled knuckles clasping tight to a purse. Her world had gotten so small by then, reduced to a closet of shoes and purses that she changed often through the days, transferring a stick of gum and Kleenex, pen and lipstick—from leather to silk to straw and back, as she relived a lifetime of various social events.

Debby remembered the times that she rummaged her mother's purses, sometimes finding things she didn't want to see. She had often reached in during church looking for a pen to draw on the bulletin. She liked to do beards and earrings on the pictured preacher and all the deacons. Sometimes she did little speech balloons and made up secret letter/number codes in which she let them say things like, *Give it to me, baby. Oh yeah,* the kinds of things she had heard on occasion from her parents' room during their big parties when she and her sisters got all dressed up and served canapés and then did a version of "So Long, Farewell" so their mother could feel like some kind of Maria von Trapp mother of the year.

In church she found hotel keys and toothpicks from a martini—faint fruity liquor traces held tight inside the lining. Lighter and cigarettes—Virginia Slims and then those long thin brown ones—Mores. "I want More," her mother said often, her comic and dramatic effect demanding the spotlight, not knowing that her desire might arrive years later in the form of lung cancer and dysfunctional children. Inside the depths of those purses was a whole warehouse of information: theater stubs, grocery bills, drugstore receipts. Even now, Debby can stand in front of her mother's closet and glimpse her own life there. The soft red calfskin purse that brushed her cheek when she grabbed her mom around the waist and begged not to be left at Bible camp. The teetering patent stiletto that she focused on when her mother bent to kiss her goodnight and that she heard clicking down the hall, as she struggled to stay awake and listen to the voices of the adults gathered in the living room to play charades long into the night.

She stands before her mother's closet, this sealed treasure like Tut's tomb of shoes and purses, and all she can think of is the miles traveled. The best article she ever wrote was experimental, a travel piece all about D.C. She was hoping to pitch it as a regular thing so she could explore new places several times a year. She did all the standard tourist stops but the focus of that piece was the Holocaust Museum because she could not stop thinking about that mountain of shoes. The orphaned objects held the memory of the person, arch to instep, leather molded to contours of flesh and bone. The click of all those heels lost to time, coming home, going to work, meeting a lover on the outskirts of town.

Sad times—lost souls, everyone looking for a good one. Everyone seeking a cobbler of the heart. She put that in the article. She also wrote that one way to determine a good soul is to imagine that there is another holocaust and that you are crippled or freckled or someone who loves monster truck pulls or has a body mass index slightly higher than average, an SAT score slightly lower, whatever the undesirable trait of the day might be, and you ask, *Will you hide me? Will you save me? Will you sacrifice your life to do so?*

The editor told her that several readers had complained that people don't want to hear sad things or take depressing trips.

"Our readers do not want questions that make them think," he said. "They just want to be entertained." He would like for her to write a piece about Disney or Six Flags or Myrtle Beach, something people can use.

DEBBY USED TO BLAME her own sadness on her childhood and a lifestyle in which the kids were secondary, like pets, a lifestyle in which someone else, usually an elderly sitter, helped out with homework, tucked them in. Debby often fantasized that she was a child growing up in what her mother called "the cracker box houses," a row of tiny mill houses out near the interstate. She knew the children who lived over there and knew people felt sorry for them. They wore hand-me-downs and got free school lunches. But she envied the freedom they seemed to have. Their parents were either not there or working too hard to monitor and comment on everything they did.

Her sisters had bought the happy picture that had been painted of their lives and even now pretend that it had been wonderful right up to the day their dad died and they discovered (and never mentioned again) that his coworker at the bank, a large coarse woman they had all referred to as Big-Butt Betty, was more than just a friend. He died young and with plenty of life insurance; Betty was not a gossip nor someone with a social life. These two facts allowed the family happiness myth to survive and even grow, becoming easier and brighter with each passing day.

Going Away Shoes

After her purses, Debby's mother loved her mink stole. She wore it to church and to cocktail parties from November to February regardless of the temperature. Then there were her shoes, of course. There was box after box of the special dyed-to-match shoes (Debby's mother made them say "peau de soie") labeled like artifacts: Engagement Shoes 1947, Wedding Shoes 1948, Cotillion 1951, Valentine Ball 1955, and so on. She loved her little Joan & Davids with the silver heels and that cute little storage bag that came with them. She once told Debby and her sisters that she wanted to be buried in the spectator pumps she wore with her Going Away Suit after the wedding. "There's still a little rice in one," she said. "Take that out when it's time." She was young when she said that, their father still alive, and even younger those afternoons when she took out all the shoes and let the girls try them on and practice walking in heels. The one childhood game they could all agree on was Cinderella as they looked for the perfect fit.

One sister, Carly, became just as obsessed with shoes as their mother and now has a closet filled herself. She owns Manolos because she wants to be Sarah Jessica Parker. Some of her shoes cost as much as a used car.

Debby has been wearing the same pair of clogs for over five years. Once sturdy and solid, they are now wearing thin, and it is that part of her—the worn-thin part—that sometimes in the midst of the oxygen sounds and murmurs from the soaps (*I don't love you anymore. But I don't understand. Bounty, the quicker picker-upper)* wants to get up and walk away from it all. It is that part of her that breathes, *Pull it, pull the plug.*

MEMORIES OF HER FATHER are dim because he didn't say much. Still, he drove them to school every morning, and there was comfort in the way he smelled of Aqua Velva and listened to the news. He was a man who knew what was happening in the world, and though their mother never listened to a word he said, Debby had felt sure that if a disaster should strike, he would know what to do. But maybe the comfort came simply from going to school. School was a haven; she loved the warm yeasty smell of those big rolls they served every single day in the cafeteria and the broad smiles and loud voices of the women back in the kitchen talking and cooking, their foreheads and underarms sweating as they talked and stirred big steaming pots of beef stew or macaroni and tomatoes.

One woman, the one who called children names like "smiley" or "curlytop" or "stinker" and who was known for giving them extra large portions of banana pudding, wore terrycloth slippers. Debby imagined a small dark bedroom where the woman rose from the warmth of her quilt-covered bed and slipped her strong sturdy feet into those worn shoes. Debby loved imagining herself in that tiny dark house with the soothing calm of the woman's voice. *Have some more pudding, smileyface,* she might say. *You haven't had near enough.*

After lunch came quiet time, when the teacher told them to rest their heads on their desks and listen to a story. She could have stayed in that pose forever. She can still sometimes take off in her mind and be somewhere else far away. It's not as easy as it was in school quiet time, but some days when there are no interruptions, she can do it. She can escape and travel for miles and miles.

> "What is it with you and the coloreds?" her mother asked on more than one occasion. "What is *that* about?"

Debby's sister Carly, who lives an hour away, leaves her engine running while she comes in to check. Debby has known herself to wish that Carly's little Miata would get stolen, but then she'd have to listen to *that* drama, and there is already so much to hear. Carly is fifty but looks about thirty because she works out several hours a day and has gone vegan. She is on her second marriage to a much younger man and just had breast-reduction surgery. The new husband likes a more "boyish and androgynous" look. She also told Debby how ironic and interesting it was because the first husband, who was *not* capable of getting her pregnant, loved breasts big enough to hide in, which is why she had gotten them enlarged twenty years before. Why she would choose to tell this is beyond Debby. The first time Debby ever heard the words *collagen* and *Botox* was right out of Carly's newly plumped and lineless lips. For the most part, Carly talks only about Carly and whatever is a natural extension of herself: her Maltese, Tipsy, or her two-year-old daughter, Mary Claire, a child Debby only really knows from various photos Carly brings—a progression from fat bald baby with what looks like a lacy pink garter on her head up to cherubic plump toddler with a very big hair bow. Mary Claire doesn't visit because Carly feels the atmosphere of sickness and impending death will scar her. Mary Claire is proof of Carly's youth and vitality.

"I'll do anything to keep you," an old anorectic-looking, liquor-swilling woman says on the television to a much younger man, who looks greasy enough to ooze. "Anything. I'm desperate." And she *is* desperate, crawling there on the floor at his feet. He says, "I don't understand," but looks at her in a way that says, *Yes, I do, and as soon as I can shed myself of her sorry ass, I'll be gone.* It's a toss-up who is the sorrier of the two, but it doesn't matter because the show goes to a commercial for a kind of shampoo that will make you orgasm in the shower. The next commercial promises that if you buy this cheese cracker over the other brand, you will be the life of the party and loved by all.

"Come join us for lunch," Debby tells Carly, but Carly wrinkles her sunburned nose and begs off because what Debby has fixed for lunch was once part of something that had eyeballs. The eggs that are now deviled and sprinkled with paprika came from a chicken, the milk from a cow. Carly complains about how the house smells. She is worried what the doctor who is a friend of the new husband will think when he makes that house call he plans to make just because of her. She is so proud of this house call, she has mentioned it nineteen times, because it will be her good deed—especially in the eyes of their other sister, Wanda—for several months if it ever happens. Wanda, the baby at forty-seven, cannot talk about anything except her son's college applications. She hires so many tutors and planners you'd think the child was some rich invalid à la *The Secret Garden*. She babbles on and on about Justin's many accomplishments while also complaining of the exertion and dedication it takes to make all of this happen. She said if it didn't take so much out of her she would do more to help at this end. Her doughy pink face is identical to their mother's thirty years ago. Her frown lines are permanently furrowed as she describes how hard it is these days to get in the really, really good schools. Since Justin was in seventh grade, she's been reading a periodical called *Ivy Search*. Her husband, Justin Sr., had (though his family has never broadcast it) a grandmother who was part Cherokee, and they are hoping to make use of this on his application. The boy can memorize and copy and rephrase anything you throw his way, but Debby has yet to hear an original idea come out of his mouth. If the topic is not something memorized in preparation for a standardized test, he seems dumb as a post. You can see his eyes glaze and jaw slacken when you ask a question he hasn't been told the answer to; he has been taught not to try unless he's absolutely sure he will get a correct score because otherwise he will lose valuable points.

Wanda is most excited about all the languages he is trying to speak—especially Russian—and during her last visit promised their unconscious mother that he would come and recite some one day as soon as they finish writing his college essay. Right after she left the crack den, Wanda used to speak in tongues and scriptures and homilies, so Russian is a huge improvement. And unlike Carly, Wanda does at least try to include Debby from time to time. Just the other month she invited her to go to the mall to get a pedicure—Wanda's treat since Debby is the *caretaker.*

For someone with such a brilliant son, and so in touch, Wanda is not always the brightest star. The Asian women running the salon were talking and laughing and Wanda whispered that it made her uncomfortable, that if Justin were here he would know what they were saying but she hadn't a clue.

"Well, I know what they're saying," Debby told her and managed to keep a straight face. "I did date a boy whose mother was Hawaiian, remember?" And of course Wanda remembered, as the family talked forever about how Debby dated a boy that was Korean or Chinese or Polynesian or something like that. Wanda did not pick up on the sarcasm in Debby's voice and instead took the reminder as proof that Debby could in fact interpret the words of the women. Wanda bit her lip and narrowed her eyes and demanded to know what they were saying. The women were still looking back and forth at each other and laughing. "Tell me," she demanded.

"I'll translate as best I can," Debby said, leaning close to whisper when the women aimed a fan at their toenails and stepped out the doorway to smoke. "But don't get upset."

"I won't. Why would I? It's not like they're writing me a letter of recommendation." She clutched the locket she always wore that had pictures of Big Justin and Little Justin inside.

"Well, the one with short hair said, 'Good God almighty, look at these ugly-ass feet.' And the other one said, 'Shit. I'd quit before I touched those things.' "

Wanda believed her, even after Debby laughed and confessed it was a joke. Debby had long wondered if a few too many brain cells got left behind in the crack den or scattered all those times Wanda fell out in a fit of evangelical ecstasy and hit her head on the floor. This confirmed it. Wanda refused to leave a tip, and when she decided she had to go back, a sacrifice made for Justin Jr. so her feet would look good when chaperoning his prom, they cut her to the quick (she said) and gave her yet another infection. Not unusual for Wanda—she has a lot of ailments, mainly the ones that have become popular, those diseases du jour that have taken the place of severe menstrual cramps and sick headaches, two ailments their mother pleaded often when she wanted sympathy and attention and/or to recline and watch the soaps all day.

"I'M GOING TO JUMP," a boozed-up broad calls from a fire escape on the television.

"You threaten it so often," a blasé man swilling a martini says, "just do it already."

And then there's a commercial. It's Friday so if she jumps no one will know what she lands on until Monday. For all we know she's on the first floor, but at this point Debby is hoping for a high-rise. Wanda says she wishes she could help this weekend but there is so much to do she is about to die from exertion and will need to check in on Monday. Wanda says she is working on learning Korean and Thai. Justin is helping her, so she can go somewhere else and get her nails done. "Like you learned from that foreign boy you dated. Koi." She says the name as if daring Debby to come back with something snappy.

"Like the fish?" her mother had asked years ago when she told them about her date, and Debby was hit with a barrage of questions that she answered as quickly and simply as possible. His name is Hawaiian. His mother is Hawaiian. No, his dad is from Charlotte. Yes, his eyes have a little bit of a slant to them. Yes, his hair is dark and straight.

"Now how are they connected to the others like the Chinese and Japanese?" Carly had asked at least seven times, until Debby finally excused herself to leave. It was not easy to do but she did. She kept her date with Koi Clark instead of driving with her mother and sisters to the outlet malls at Myrtle Beach. But later, by the time they finished quizzing her about Koi and telling her what she had missed and how much easier it would have been on everyone if she had driven them because her car had the biggest trunk and how it was the last time they had a little happy group outing *before daddy died*, she was sorry she had kept the date. The price paid for that trip to the movies with a nice person she would likely never see again was too high.

There was a time when anything but white-bread mainstream was a joke in their house, even if now Wanda is desperate to become Miss Multicultural. When Debby did date a white-bread product, Troy Preston, star halfback and son of the town's leading surgeon, they didn't understand that, either—meaning, of course, that they didn't understand what he saw in her.

Break the chain. Pull the plug—pull it, pull it.

One person Debby did care about enough to call him her boyfriend happened to be black. She and Ronnie were the best fencers in the small junior college they attended. Actually they were the *only* fencers—part of a small intramural experiment—and not very good, either of them. They would meet in the gym several afternoons a week to joust about, the only sounds being the squeak of their shoes on the blond polished wood and their rhythmic breathing as they circled each other in a kind of dance. One day, walking back to their dorms, they talked about how the thing they liked most of all in fencing was the mask, that it was like peering out a dark screen door. Their bodies were outside, moving in the world, while their souls remained hidden. It was a beautiful October day and the clarity of the colors and brisk chilly air made Debby almost giddy, more talkative than she had ever been. It prompted her to lean in close enough that their arms brushed and their hands naturally found each other, their fingers locked tight for that five-minute stroll as they continued discussing their sport. They liked to lunge forward, swords crossed as they pressed their weight against each other, struggling to make eye contact and hold it. There was a connection she hadn't felt before and hasn't in all the years since. They were all for one and one for all.

Ronnie once asked, midlunge, eyes safe behind his mask, if it bothered her that he was black. "No," she said, "does it bother you I'm not?" He pressed in closer. Her wrist bent, giving, and he pinned her against the concrete wall, both their swords raised overhead, and pressed his mouth against hers through the masks. The mesh of their face guards was metallic and cold, a reminder of time and place and the coach just inside the glass office door.

"We're a good fit," he told her the one time she allowed him to stay in her room through the night. Stretched side by side, their bodies matched up, hipbones and ankles, elbows and shoulders. Ronnie wasn't tall but people often asked, *Does he play basketball? Can he do the moonwalk?* And once recently, Carly asked about his *size*. "You know," she said and giggled, caressing her hair newly dyed a shade of red that does not exist in nature. Debby hoped that her silence left all kinds of questions for Carly to mull over, but in five minutes Carly was completely immersed in telling a story about someone she knew who had had her eyeliner tattooed on even though the procedure is illegal now. Though Debby would never tell Carly or anyone else, the truth was memories of Ronnie and what it was like to be with him had for years played in her mind like a backbeat, the bass rhythm of what she wanted in life, a kind of person, a kind of relationship, a kind of freedom and security system all rolled into one.

While her sisters go on and on about their latest interactions with their mother, telling whoever visits what they have done and "what mother said," Debby wants to point out that they're talking about a woman whose last truly alert moments were about two months ago when there was a naked clown living in her closet. He came out in the middle of the night and told her to take all of her clothes off, which is why Debby was finding her all tangled up and half naked each morning. Their mother said he should have been ashamed saying and doing all those things he did but she did have to chuckle over it all. He was a clown after all, even if he did bear a striking resemblance to that awful fat woman who used to work with their dear darling daddy. By then she loved to tell all about when she first met their father, how he fell madly in love with her and was still consumed with his passion for her as he drew his last breath.

HER SISTERS LIVE in soap opera time and forget from one day to the next exactly what has happened. They have friends who change partners as often as underwear, but as soon as the recessional march plays and they are out at the reception drinking champagne and eating little finger foods, that's old news. They forget how they fucked first this one and then that one. Talked about this one, lied about that one. They forget because life is just so hard—so hard to get Justin in an Ivy and so hard to satisfy a husband while also satisfying yourself. So hard to find a good hair color person or a housekeeper or Russian tutor or pedicurist. They forget their dad was in love with Big-Butt Betty or that Uncle Ted and the sex-convention women flew too close to the sun, that Wanda once lived in a crack den and that Carly's whole life has been dictated by her boobs and how the men she married have ordered her to wear them. Her sisters forget because it's easier that way.

They will, however, never forget that Debby has dated people of different colors and they will never forget the time she wore white shoes after Labor Day. She was only twenty-five and had fractured her toe, and those were the only shoes that could accommodate a great big bandage. Still, they were embarrassed and ashamed. They talked about it and talked about it, their mother saying how surely she had taught Debby better than that! It all gets regularly visited, too, the white shoes and Koi and Ronnie, though the years have led them to call him Rashad.

"Debby was international before international was cool," Justin's dad, Justin, says, standing tall in his shiny conservative shoes. They will remember those goddamned white shoes and her one real boyfriend (because he was black and not because he was nice) when all that's left on earth are Tupperware products and the cockroaches.

SOMETIMES, WHEN IT'S too late for a sisterly drive-by, Debby sits in that room with all the power of malicious force. She could withhold food and drink. She could accidentally trip and pull the oxygen plug. *She* could smoke long brown cigarettes and fill the room with carbon monoxide. But why? No one can give her an edited rerun, a return to the choices she didn't make. No one can give her a second chance with Ronnie, the nerve to get in a car or on the bus and go when he invited her to come see him after he transferred to Furman. She told him her sister was getting married and she needed to be there to help (true); she told him her mother was having a memorial service on the anniversary of her father's death (true); she told him she was sick, and she was. Sick with fear and lack of courage and the price tag of her own freedom. *Pull it. Pull the plug.* And then another year passed with an invitation she didn't have the nerve to accept and then too many years passed and thoughts of Ronnie were replaced with those of places that she might go. She has read so much about certain places that she feels she's been there and can play through it like memory on demand. She is on a remote country road in Scotland, surrounded by heather and shaggy wild ponies. Enormous stone castles emerge from the distant mist. Or she is stretched out on the pink sand of Bermuda, the ocean lulling her into sleep, or she is at the wailing wall, fingertips brushing the rough surface where strips of paper—desires and pleas and blessings—are rolled and tucked and crammed and hidden, whole lives pressed into cracks and crevices, or she is stretched out on a dorm bed hours from home, thoughts of graduate school and published articles and trips to Europe and Egypt and Alaska put aside while she wraps her legs around the strong young body on top of her, the pulse of his neck against her cheek, and moves against him as if her life depends on it.

A WOMAN ON TELEVISION is crying hysterically because the baby she has pretended was hers is not. "I couldn't have one," she sobs. "I am so much older than I look."

"But I don't understand," the bewildered husband says, and then there is a commercial where a happy family goes to Disney

World and meets Cinderella. *Pull it.* And then there is a man talking about his erectile dysfunction and what a drag it was but now he is all better (wife grinning in the background) and others can be back in the game, too (he throws a long football pass to a man eager for the information), "Just ask your doctor." The woman on television is still hysterical and will be for days to come until given a sedative or slapped in the face. The actor who plays the hysterical woman has a real life elsewhere. And here—in Debby's real life—she is taking care of her mother. A woman who loved purses and parties and raised her own children exactly as she had been raised. A vibrant force to rival any of those on the soaps, reduced by time—real time—to a pale, lifeless creature.

Sometimes, Debby wishes for the end. She thinks of packing a bag and calling up one of her sisters to say that she is going on that cruise. Bring over that money they have been promising her all these years. Pick up some Depends on the way. Depends, Ensure, talcum powder and lotions so she doesn't get bedsores, those new little Oral B things that fit on the fingertip so they can gently clean her slowly rotting gums. She thinks of going out for her walk and never coming back. She could reach her mile and a half marker at the elementary school and instead of turning and heading back down the street just keep going. She could get in her car and be on the interstate within minutes.

It never fails. When she gets to this point, her heart pumping with anticipation, a loud sigh will come or her mother will cry out, her eyes fixed on the spot where Peppy slept for seventeen years. And Debby will race to find her, this old wasted stranger, eyes open but distant—pale blue and alarmed, like the time they had the car accident and she held Debby's hand and stroked her hair while the emergency crew worked to unpin her from the passenger seat, the way she looked one brief moment the week after Debby's father died when she said she wished she had loved him better, or the time last year when she saw Debby packing a bag and in a wild childish way begged her please not to leave. "You're the one I have always known I could count on," she whispered.

Pack a bag. Pull the plug. Take your turn.

She is Sisyphus. All day long she pushes that rock, and when she is almost to the top, something happens to distract her, and it all rolls back to the very place the journey began. Someday she will make it to the top. Some perfect day she will stand, wind in her face, and watch the rock barrel down the other side, taking anything and anybody in its path. But until then she will travel this worn and familiar road, sure-footed and steady in real time, eyes vigilantly focused on the life before her. She is the cobbler of her own heart, and this will save her soul.

SURRENDER

THE CHILD HAD SPENT the afternoon drawing pictures of her grandmother without clothes on, and now Rose was sick and tired of it. She hadn't wanted to keep the child to begin with but what was she to do? Who could help that her son had impregnated and then married someone who was hysterical and self-centered—a horrible combination—with rings on all her fingers and her eyes drawn out like Cleopatra on the make, and who could help that her son on an average sunny Tuesday morning in October would do what he did every weekday morning, climb poles for the power company, checking and repairing lines, only to die suddenly with no warning whatsoever. For years Rose had feared he'd get electrocuted, and that was, in the darkest recesses of her mind, the call that she had dreaded getting—a bolt of lightning, a surge of power—but instead it was his heart, an inner surge and sudden shock that left him slumped and tethered to a pole until a coworker who was sitting in the truck eating breakfast happened to glance up a second time to note that Drew's position had not changed at all, that it was not a game. "Too late," was what the EMT person said. "Nothing anyone could've done."

The coworker, a friend of Drew's since high school, where they had both excelled as athletes and class clowns, confided—*confessed*—that the long minutes he had sat there eating his Egg McMuffin he had been laughing at what Drew was famous for doing, a kind of lewd pole dance, pressing his pelvis against gummy creosote, his spiked boots kicked and swung outward, hard hat tipped seductively to one side, to entertain his buddies down below. All those minutes just hanging there.

It would be easier if it had come from the outside, if the world had betrayed him instead of his own body. He had inherited a family history of high blood pressure and heart disease that ran through her veins. Hank gave him long muscular legs and a face almost too sweet to be handsome, one that would have benefited from the creases and lines of age. She gave him poor vision and heart disease. She betrayed him every time she had ever fed him his favorite deep-fried foods and butter- and sugar-filled desserts, by never saying a word about his chain smoking and beer drinking, the growing pudge around his middle, grown considerably pudgier since marrying a girl who never cooked anything but fast food in a microwave and whose idea of a vegetable was the flat thin pickle on a cheeseburger.

And now here Rose sat with what was left of her son, a five-year-old girl with spiky short hair, an awful haircut attempting to correct what the child had done to herself with a pair of manicuring scissors locked right there in Rose's own bathroom just two days after Drew died. The child's green eyes—slit like a cat's—stayed fixed on Rose while the girl drew yet another picture of exposed breasts. The pictures were harsh and smudged where her plump sticky hands smeared the page and then the cream-colored carpet. She colored in the nipples this time with green crayon, all the while studying everything Rose did. Rose thought that something was wrong with the child even before Drew died and now she was sure of it, though Hank said that that was nonsense. "In fact," Hank had said just last night, "I think she's a lot like Drew."

Now Rose turned, hands clasped tightly to squelch her desire to grab and twist that dimpled sunburned arm. "Stop that," she said through gritted teeth, surprised herself by the harshness of the sound. "Stop."

"My mama said I can draw." The child stared back without blinking, stuck out her tongue but then licked her lips like that was all she meant to do.

"So fine. Draw. But don't draw me." Before Rose could even turn away, the child had reached for a new piece of paper and begun again. She always gave Rose an enormous nose and mouth and then itty-bitty eyes, and that was what she was working on first—little red eyes, like a pig's, in a massive moon face. How would Hank handle this when it was his turn to tend to her? He agreed before Rose could even open her mouth that the child could stay with them anytime at all, making it sound like they could run a twenty-four-hour daycare center, and now where was he but off running errands, getting fence supplies, dog food, something good for supper "to go with the surprise I've got your grandma baking just for you," he had told the child, leaving her to clap her hands and dance around before settling back into her demon-driven drawing. Hank was good for his word. He would come home having done a lot, but he would have also taken his time, riding along in the sunshine with some country music station playing. That left arm of his stayed mighty tan, proof of all those hours he hit the back roads. He called it his "meditation time," and there was a part of her that envied his ability to so easily calm and collect himself even through the worst and most frightening times. Still, he wasn't there for the art gallery of nudity, and she was.

"Some people call these nursers," the child said and pointed to the purple circled breasts she had drawn. Rose's hair looked like a rat's nest in this particular drawing and the child had put two dark little horns there on the top of her head. "Some people say titties, bosoms, boobies."

"Well, I say stop!" Rose put down the book she had tried unsuccessfully to read all day long, a book about learning patience and forgiveness, but so far she hadn't been able to concentrate on a goddamn bit of it. "What kind of girl are you, anyway?"

"I'm not a girl."

Sweet Jesus. Last week the child had pretended to be a pony and whinnied and trotted and carried on all day long, snorting and stomping, eating only carrots and licking sugar right off the dining room table where she had poured herself a little pile from the sugar bowl. She would not listen to Rose unless Rose called her My Little Pony, and then she'd stop as if perking her ears, cocking her head first one way and then the other.

When Drew was little he had pretended to be Lassie, Rin Tin Tin, Bullet. His child bride probably didn't know any of those things about him and how could she? She was half his age and half his intelligence. All those years Rose and Hank had watched him go through girlfriend after girlfriend, many of them perfectly lovely and fine, wondering when he'd ever settle down, and then this was it. Forget birth control and have yourself a wedding. He met her line dancing for God's sake and the boy had never liked to dance in his whole life. And then here she was, this girl whose big ambition in life was to get to be social coordinator for the clerical staff down at Toyota, where she worked as a receptionist. A girl who liked to give cute little titles and names to everything as if her experience walking the earth was so unique and almighty important it had to be documented. She referred to where she sat there by the automatic door of the Toyota showroom as "my Toyota throne," as if she ruled over the whole dealership kingdom. She called her car "Backfire Betty" and she called Drew "my maverick man," in a way that dripped with sexual residue, right there in Rose's living room. It was like the girl was mentally stuck in adolescence probably drawing little hearts over her *i*'s and naming various body parts.

Drew used to follow Rose from room to room, pant and bark, lick her hand. He liked to circle and circle like their old sheltie did before flopping down and pretending to sleep. Sometimes she lifted and carried him to bed that way, plopping him down like a lump of dead weight on the bedspread. He'd let her get all the way to the door and then set in whimpering like the last mongrel left at the pound, knowing that she would never leave him that way, that she would return to tell a story or to bring him some milk, stroke his head and ears as if he really were a dog until his make-believe growls and snores lapsed into the breath of a sleeping boy.

But this child was nothing like Drew.

"She needs to be seeing a doctor," Rose said just yesterday when the child's mama showed up an hour later than she'd said, her skirt too short for anybody other than a Barbie doll or Hooters waitress or whore. "She needs to be talking and getting some help."

"Why do you think so?" The girl's eyes widened in a way that accentuated the dark circles below even though she had caked on plenty of makeup in an attempt to hide them.

"Her daddy died? She thinks she's a horse?" Rose drew a deep breath. She had worked as an administrative assistant out at County Mental Health for years and had picked up a lot of information along the way. "She draws people naked. No respect."

"She's a kid. And yeah, it's a real hard time." She had Drew's wedding ring strung around her neck on what looked like a piece of rawhide, her fingers clutching and rubbing it the whole time she talked. "If you didn't get so upset with her, she might quit."

"Let her draw you then."

"I do. She likes drawing my scar from where she was born." She rubbed her hand over her abdomen and Rose was afraid for a minute that she was going to show it. "She loved Drew's scar that went up his shin. She liked to call it "Daddy's little street.'"

Rose couldn't bear to think of Drew's scar, especially as "Daddy's little street"; just the mention of that scar made her shudder. She had been with him when it happened, there at the community center, where he was playing with a bunch of kids, running around the big L-shaped pool even though they'd been asked not to over and over by the lifeguards. "Horseplay," they called it. No running and no horseplay. She was standing in the three-foot area with some other women, their bodies oiled in Hawaiian Tropic, heads tied in bandanas. One of the women was telling about the affair she had had, how she never in a million years would have believed that she would do such a thing and yet there she was doing it, all the while thinking that life was just too short not to do it, all the while feeling like she was being pulled by an unseen force, something completely beyond her will and control. The woman confessed, too, that it was a lot easier knowing her husband had already cheated on her at least once. Rose had sometimes wondered if Hank was happy with her. Was it enough that they sank there side by side, hip bones brushing, at the end of a long day? Was it enough that they made an annual pilgrimage to some godforsaken Civil War battlefield instead of one of those romantic-sounding trips all these other people seemed to crave? Luaus on islands she would hesitate even to pronounce, bed-and-breakfasts where you paid a lot of money to share a bathroom and eat breakfast with strangers. It made her anxious that her friend had had an affair, not to mention sleeping there in a bed-and-breakfast in Asheville, and it was in the midst of all these facts and details and wonderings that she felt a surge of panic. She felt it rise through her body, adrenaline pumping, and it was beforehand—a premonition, that split second between lightning flash and the deafening sound of thunder—so that she looked up and was already moving slow motion through the water to the ladder when Drew went down stomach first with another boy, sliding over the concrete, his forward motion slowed and then stopped by a rusted metal wire at the base of the chain-link fence. Her vision blurred from sun, chlorine, a flood of fear as she watched a young frightened teenager leap from the lifeguard stand and try to remove the wire. She had never seen so much blood, the bone-white line up his leg that dotted and then filled suddenly, spreading around him in a pool on the wet concrete. She didn't even remember riding to the hospital, a different lifeguard driving, Drew's head in her lap in the backseat, leg elevated and pulsing through the large beach towel already soaked. Over a hundred stitches and hours later, they waited for Hank to arrive and drive them home. It was a beautiful day, clear sky and low humidity. Drew was telling the whole story like a battlefield account to anyone who might want to listen, what he felt, what he remembered, how many stitches, how much blood, how his mother threw up three times while he was being stitched. She focused on the sun setting over the pines and she listened to the whir of the inground sprinklers of the hospital lawn, how they arced a fine misted spray in near silence and then returned with a harsh low grinding sound only to then release and once again go easy. Soft and then harsh and then again and again.

"Do you have a door like my mama?" Now the child pressed on Rose's stomach and then with no warning lifted her shirt and pressed that damp sticky hand against Rose's flesh. "I needed the front door to get out. Right here near your winkie."

"That's a navel."

"It's a winkie."

"There's no such thing as a winkie."

"Yeah there is, too." She pulled up her own shirt and stuck her finger in her navel. "This is my winkie and that," she reached one finger and poked at Rose, "is your winkie." The child put her hands on her hips and twisted back and forth, made little *nana-nananana* sounds. "And *you* don't even have a front door."

"No I don't."

"My daddy said I was important." The child spit the word at Rose, a black permanent marker clutched in her hand. "I got my *own* door just for *me*."

"Well, good for you."

"So how did my daddy get out then?"

"Lord." Rose pulled away and walked over to the window hoping to see Hank's truck in the drive. "Who's minding the shop?" he used to ask in those early years when something went wrong—a pot of rice burned and stuck, a bill forgotten, a bag of trash left where a dog could get in it. But he hadn't used the phrase since that day Drew got hurt when she used it to berate herself again and again. And now it seemed he was overprotective about all their belongings to a degree that preoccupied his every moment. He couldn't bear to lose anything, not an old mangy barn cat, or a plant to the cold, not a dime on the floor. Nothing made him angrier than to lose his train of thought.

"My daddy probably come out the back door," the child said.

"*Came* out the back door," Rose corrected, horrified that she was even participating in this discussion.

"Women have three different doors, you know." The child waited, testing her. The marker was now uncapped, strong fumes that probably weren't good for a child to breathe all day long.

"Why don't you go see what's on television?" Rose asked, desperate to escape. Hank had promised the child monkey bread and he would be disappointed if Rose didn't fix it. "I'll get you a snack."

"I drew a picture of your door," she said and rifled through that stack of messy papers. "Grown-ups have hair, you know." She pulled out a page and Rose stared back in shock. A tangle of purple atop two orange stick legs, legs too thin to ever support the enormous mouth and breasts that filled most of the page. "I drew your fanny, too."

Rose turned back to the window, wondering what Hank would do with this. She thought of the way he cradled and carried Drew in from the car that day after the accident. He placed him on the sofa in the den and they brought him milk shakes and cookies and comic books. He wanted Kentucky Fried Chicken for dinner and she drove across town herself and waited in line, noticing only then in a warped chrome reflection that her sneakers were all bloodstained and that mascara streaks smeared her cheeks like war paint. She tried to change the bandage the first time and got so lightheaded she had to call Hank to help her. The long scar stayed white, so noticeable in the summer against his olive skin and the dark hairs of his legs. Drew loved to roll up his pants and show it, to tell the story, Rose wincing every time.

"Do you have a boo-boo place?" the child asked, and Rose shook her head, thinking, *Not really, not one that you can see.* "Does he?" she pointed to a photograph of Hank on the shelf. He was young then, bare chested and leaning up against that old blue Ford he had when she first met him—smooth, flat stomach—no trace of the emergency appendectomy he had the summer before they got married. She liked to trace her finger over the slick shiny skin, stretched tight and hardened. It reminded her of the silver trail of a slug, like the one the child had delighted in a week ago when a neighbor kid from across the street, a ten-year-old who dressed like she might be seventeen, tried to talk the child into pouring salt on the creature so they could watch it shrivel up. The child was intrigued right up to the moment the salt shaker was raised, and then she fell all to pieces, throwing her body over the slug like a shield and screaming, "He's mine, he's mine."

The child's mother did something very similar at the funeral. She crumpled there in front of half the town and squatted by the grave, the box of ashes in her arms. Rose had to look away then. Some part deep within said she should move forward, to touch and comfort. The girl had no family to speak of—an old father in a veteran's home somewhere and a sister who left early during the graveside service to catch her flight to Texas. Drew had told them that he wanted her to feel like she had a real family. He called her his "little orphan girl," "my waifish wife, my little discard." Hank had moved close and knelt there beside her, his arm around her shoulders, but Rose was frozen. Instead she looked out at the pines, at the bright cloudless sky; she focused on the sound of cars on the interstate, the rise and fall, near and then far, as rhythmic as the ocean. Now there was a jet stream across the sky, the child there beside her as she stared out the kitchen window, waiting for Hank.

"Surrender Dorothy," the child said and cackled. "Surrender, surrender, surrender, you . . ." she hesitated before calling Rose the Wicked Witch of the West, which she had done once before, something the child's mother actually reprimanded her for. "Give me my ruby slippers or this house will fall and kill you," she shrieked, and for a split second, the child did look like Drew. It was the mouth, the tilt of her head. She looked like Drew, who looked like Hank, who looked like his father before him.

"You will die!" The child pointed her finger at Rose and then ran back to her pile of papers and began scribbling furiously. Witches' hats and brooms and then breasts. Rose's breasts. Rose's mouth and nose were more distorted than ever in these new drawings. She drew little speech balloons and then scratched marks back and forth while saying, "I'll get you. I'll get you, your dog, too."

"Quit goddamnit." Rose knelt and leaned down to make eye contact. She wanted to grab the child but was afraid if she did, if she ever gripped those little arms and began shaking, she might not be able to stop. "Do you hear? Do you? Leave me alone." Her words came in jerks, loud harsh syllables.

The child's gaze never broke, her hand grasping a black marker. She drew two big circles, dotted the centers like fried eggs. Circle dot. Circle dot. Then the child started laughing hysterically. She threw herself on her back, legs cycling the air to show the filthy marker-stained bottom of her worn-out shorts. Mucous and tears smeared her face, and the more she laughed, the more tightly her eyes closed, mouth twisted, the more she looked like Drew all those times he got out of control at church or a ceremony of some sort, all those places he should've been behaving and couldn't help himself. She thought of him then in a way she hadn't in years, there at a high school awards banquet when they served what he had always called "fanny rolls" for obvious reasons, twin mounds of golden bread. Drew raised and held up his roll, there at the head table, where he was about to be named athlete of the year, and audibly called out, "Mom, Dad, check it out." And then he became hysterical, running his finger along the crack of the roll, whispering to his friends, who then joined in with their own jokes, getting more and more rowdy and out of control. Drew kept on until iced tea ran from his nostrils and the whole table full of great big boys and a couple of cheerleaders had to excuse themselves to go outdoors and regain composure. For years he was misbehaving and laughing that way and then all of a sudden it slowed down, not much, but a little. The slowing seemed to coincide with his new life, the girl, the child on the way.

When Drew brought the child's mother home to meet them, Rose was shocked. What did this say about her as a mother? Wouldn't a boy pick someone like his mother if it were a good relationship? Her opposite if there were problems? The girl showed up for a Saturday night cookout with just the three of them looking like she was going to the queen's coronation.

"What does this say about what he thinks of me?" Rose asked Hank late that night when they were in bed, her head still filled with a perfume too musky even for the horniest wild creature.

"Nothing. It isn't about you," he said. Of course he hadn't even noticed how inappropriate she looked. Only that she seemed shy and uncomfortable when Rose started asking questions about her parents.

"I asked important questions," Rose said. "Family history is important. And I'd think he'd want someone more like me."

"Who says she isn't like you?" He laughed and then reached over to pull her close. "Maybe it's only boys who are unhappy with their moms who try to duplicate so they can try again to make everything okay." He barely paused so she wouldn't have time to speak, time to ask just what daytime talk show he'd been watching. "Maybe," he continued, his hand gripping and rocking her hipbone, "you're such a good mother he can just follow his most natural desires."

"Or lust."

"Okay, lust. What's wrong with a little lust?" He slid his hand along her side, thumb circling and stroking her breast through the thin cotton of her gown. "C'mon," he whispered. "Give it a chance."

That's what he said these days about the child, too. *Give her a chance.* But that's not always easy to do with her sitting there like a hysterical little devil cat hell-bent on aggravating her grandmother.

"Some boobies is great big," she said as soon as Rose looked her way. "Yours ain't so big."

Now Rose longed for Drew. She longed for Hank. She wanted back all those times it was just the three of them. If she had ever known all that was coming she would have done so many things differently. She would have made him go to the doctor more often and she would have stressed a healthier diet and years before she would not have allowed him to engage in horseplay at all. She would have stayed in his room just a few minutes longer those nights he fell asleep pretending to be a dog. She would have nursed him a few months longer, not rushed in those wee morning hours to get back to bed herself but just sat there holding him, making it all last. Maybe the three of them would have gone on vacation someplace foreign and exotic where they wouldn't have known the language and wouldn't have cared.

And yet, Hank had pointed out when she expressed some of these longings, usually in the dark, often when she thought he was sleeping, she couldn't have nursed Drew forever—he did grow teeth—and there was no way to keep him from goofing around the way he did, and look at what they would have lost if they'd guarded him so—a fun-loving and good-hearted man adored by hundreds of people. And Drew was okay with the trips they did take. Sliding Rock was fun, wasn't it? Six Flags over Georgia. Fort Fisher.

Whether or not Drew really loved the old Civil War battlefields the same way Hank did was something she would now never know. What she did know is that they spent hours talking about it, and Drew encouraged Hank's idea to step foot on every battlefield he could. Hank decided to make it part of his birthday, even kept a little scrapbook of it all with postcards and notes: Shiloh at fifty, Gettysburg just last month when he turned sixty-five, lots of little battles Rose had never heard of there in between. She went with him to Gettysburg, an experience she had not been able to shake in the days since, a host of sighs and shadows. She felt that in cemeteries sometimes. A still moment when the wind became language—giving in, giving up, giving—and there were prayers and murmurs, grief and desire all run together in a whooshing sound like the ocean, like ultrasound, the baby's heart submerged there in the womb, floating peacefully, little dinghy bumping the dock. She was Drew's dock, and there was, had always been, an invisible line tethering mother to child—a single cry in the dark night and her breasts tightened with a surge, the phantom sensation of milk about to flow even years after when there was nothing there to give.

She had waited these long weeks to hear Drew's voice. She thought it would come in a dream. In a word. Now she realized the child's mother was in the kitchen doorway watching her, and Rose had no idea how long she had been standing there. Monkey bread. She had begun the process without even paying attention, biscuits taken from the roll and dipped in milk, rolled in sugar and cinnamon, tossed in a Bundt pan with butter in between. Hank had promised the child monkey bread and she did what all children do, pictured a loaf shaped like a monkey, long dangling arms or wings and little caps like the ones from *The Wizard of Oz* she liked to mimic. He explained to her that it got its name because that's how you eat it, like little monkeys, using your hands to pick and pull. "We'll act like monkeys," he promised her and scratched under his arms before catching her up in a big strong hug, something he seemed to have no trouble doing.

"Drew always wanted me to make that," she said. "He wanted me to ask you about it."

"Really."

"He said one of his favorite memories is when you acted like a monkey. And of course the way you let him act like a dog, licking his plate and scratching his ear with his foot." She paused but Rose did not look up. She stared at the biscuits in her hand, damp lumps of dough and sugar. "He said sometimes *he* gave *you* commands. Things like shake, roll over, play dead." They both froze, the word lingering heavy in the air around them. "Drew said y'all laughed all the time. He said he wanted to give me that kind of life."

What kind of life? she wanted to ask, starved for the words she was hearing, but instead she said, "I haven't made this silly bread in years." She said, "It's terrible for you, too. Pure sugar and starch."

"I found Molly a day care place," she said. "I'm sorry if she's been in the way." Then the child was there, handing her mother a stack of the drawings she had produced through the course of the long day. She held up one where you couldn't tell Rose's mouth from her breast but the intention of her focus was clear all the same.

"Stop it, now," Drew's wife said. "Your grandma doesn't like that."

"Here's her nursers."

"Stop it, Molly."

"Titties."

"Please. We need to go."

"No. I want the monkey food."

"We'll come back."

"No," the child screamed. "He said she'd cook it just for me and now she is. And," she pulled out another piece of paper and waved it in the air, "here's her big fanny."

"That's it." Drew's wife was crying then as she bent and wrestled the squirming child into her arms. "I've had it."

"It's okay," Rose said, watching them, her own chest tight with longing. Drew's wife was wearing one of his old T-shirts and it dwarfed her small frame. She clutched the child with one arm, and her free hand held the string around her neck as if it held all that Drew had promised her. A family. Laughter. A lifetime of love. "I do have a big fanny," Rose said. "I really do." The child's loud mischievous laugh filled the room. She wiggled out of her mother's arms and ran up to Rose, stopping just shy of their bodies touching. She raised her small hand and held it up in front of Rose's breast as if daring Rose to do something.

"That's my breast," Rose said, wiping her sticky hands with a dishtowel.

"Nurser," the child said, looking up and leaning in so close Rose could feel her breath.

"My nurser."

"Tittie." She reached and pressed Rose's breast, leaving marker smudge on the pocket of her shirt.

"Molly." Drew's wife straightened up and then reached in and grabbed the child's hand, twisted, and yanked her away.

"Tittie, say it." The child was torn then between laughing and crying, her face flushed as she tried to shake loose her mother's grip.

Out the window, Rose saw Hank walking up from the mailbox, a sack of Purina over his shoulder; he loped along engaged in the world in a way few people are. Even the retrievers bouncing and barking along didn't seem to faze him. Her heart filled with the sight of him there, a flow of blood coursing through her veins, and where did it come from? This feeling? This urgency?

"Quit it." Drew's wife wiped her cheeks as she spoke, her voice filled with exhaustion. "Please."

"Not till she says it."

"Tittie," Rose said then. "Tittie and nurser and tittie again." She touched the child's head, petted down a piece of sticky spiked hair. She held her open palm up to Drew's wife to tell her to stay, to wait, *please don't leave,* and some part of her wanted to linger there, to put her arm around the girl's shoulders—her name was Melinda—to put her arm around Melinda's shoulders the way that Hank had done. To hug the child—Drew's child, Molly—close to her chest. But first she had to get to the door, then she would be right back. She would take the hot sweet bread from the oven and she would find a chain for the ring around

Melinda's neck, some clean shorts for Molly, but right now she could not get to the door fast enough. She was moving through the house then, her hands grasping the tops of tables and the backs of chairs—her hands leaving traces of sugar and flour, prints, traces of all their hands through all the years. And of course she would hear her son again. She would always hear him. There in the darkness, a pant and a whimper, a sigh and a whisper, the softest breath of a windless night as she lay waiting for sleep, Hank there by her side, and now she could not get to him fast enough.

MIDNIGHT CLEAR

"WHAT MAKES THIS night different from all the rest?" Charles asks. His hair is damp with sleep as he follows me from room to room, a crumbling graham cracker in one sticky hand and a glass of chocolate milk in the other. He is five. His brother, Michael, who is eight, is absorbed in the Game Boy he holds in his hand, a series of beeps and distracting sounds. He is also watching cartoons and moving one bare foot under the edge of the rug in a way that flips it and scatters dust and crumbs about every thirty seconds. The other question Charles has asked ten times since waking from his nap is how Santa Claus comes out of a wood-burning stove. "Won't that hurt?" he asks. "What if he wants to give me something big?" This one got his brother's attention. He has figured everything out about Santa Claus, you can see it in his eyes, but is not yet ready to admit the truth. Once the truth is admitted, there's no taking it back, no return to what you once believed in so completely. You would think that those early experiences of disappointment and loss and disillusionment would prepare us for what lies ahead. Things like career disappointments, a parent dying way too young, a marriage that functions the way a mirage does, constantly forcing physical distance so you can continue to see something that isn't really there.

It is Christmas Eve—our first in this new house, our first in our new family configuration—a single mother and two young sons. Charles has already taken the little figure of Joseph out of the crèche several times and placed him at the far end of the table with a green Matchbox car that resembles the one his dad drives. "You live over here now," I have heard him say and then nod and giggle as if the little plastic Joseph had just told him a joke. "You're still my daddy," he says, a recital of all he has heard during the past eleven months. He has claimed the Jesus figure as his own namesake and a little plastic Spiderman figure as his brother. I, of course, am Mary and keep finding my figure placed outside of the manger, close enough to see what is going on but out of the building nonetheless. "You are working in the yard," he has told me. "You are at the grocery store and will be right back."

WHAT MAKES THIS NIGHT different from all the rest? Well, the divorce would be the biggest difference. That and the fact that I invited their dad and their dad's parents and even their dad's new girlfriend to stop by for drinks in less than eight hours. And now I'm wondering why I ever did such a stupid thing. Because it's the season of giving and forgiving? Because all the books say that kids need both parents, that if a parent is cut away from the child's life it should be because the child decided to do it and not because one parent orchestrates it or poisons thoughts and feelings? Like all those times I have almost by accident swept Joseph and his little sports car into the garbage only to fish him out, wipe stuff like macaroni and cheese off of him, and place him back before Charles notices.

The boys have told me that the girlfriend, Nanci, has two broken arms and talks without moving her lips. Whether these attributes are related I have no idea, and true to what all the books advise, I have not asked any questions. I am assuming she was in a bad accident. Or maybe she's a ventriloquist who fell down a flight of stairs. She might not have even broken them at the same time. The second break could have been the result of trying to cater to the first.

When they talk about Nanci, I can't help but feel responsible. I wished for her after all. When the marriage counselor, after months of dead-end conversations and stalemates—hour after hour of white noise and Kleenex boxes and that pasture full of dead horses we regularly flogged—asked what I really wanted, I stared out his window where I had watched a weeping willow move from icy tendrils to bright green and back again and thought: *Out.* I just wanted out. And it was at that moment I began wishing that he would meet somebody—anybody—so the path to the exit sign might be a little easier.

I told the therapist that what I wanted more than anything was a dog that didn't pee in the house, a dog who knew to walk right up to the door and beg to *get out.* My attempt at making a subtle point was lost to inarticulate execution.

So, WHAT MAKES this night different? It hits me when I open the back door to take out the trash. It smells like shit. Literally. The smell of raw sewage fills the air. Charles drops the cracker to the floor so he can hold his nose, which pleases Beau, our sweet but incontinent basset hound, who lumbers over to clean up. "Beau," Charles reprimands and shoves the tired old dog with his foot. "You stink." But it's not Beau and I know that. I stare out at the rectangle of dead grass where the thin layer of snow melted as soon as it hit. I have lived here almost a year and know nothing about the septic tank. Just as I knew nothing about the sag in the foundation that needed to be jacked up, the old termite damage to one edge of the porch, the faulty wiring in the storage room, and the dryer vent that did not meet code.

How big could the problem be?

I have come to expect very big. I have come to think that odds are it will be every bit as bad as it can be, and if for some reason it isn't, then I should rush right out and buy a lottery ticket and dash to the frozen-food section of the grocery where *they* say you are likely to meet nice intelligent and normal people. "And who are *they*?" I ask my mother and all other well-meaning advice givers. *They* also say that church is a good place to meet people. However, *they* don't offer to keep your children or tell you what to do with them while you are out going to all these places.

"Do you want some matzo?" Charles asks Beau and lures the tired soul back into the kitchen. "Do you want some eggnog?" Charles has been hooked on Passover—food and litany—ever since attending a Seder last spring. It was the longest meal of my life. The host asked the children, "Why is this night different from all the rest?" But really, what all the adults wanted to know and weren't asking was, *What really happened to your marriage?* The four real questions had nothing to do with why we were eating bread that tasted like cardboard and chewing on bitter herbs, double-dipping and reclining while eating. The questions that came to me in hushed whispers or innuendo were: *Is there a chance of reconciliation? Is there someone else involved? Can you afford it financially?* And the most common of all: *But really, how are you?* Sometimes with the stress on *are* and sometimes with the stress on *you*, always delivered with great pity.

Elijah's wine goblet stayed empty because I kept drinking up whatever was allotted the ghostly guest. I figured if Elijah has half a brain then he knows I needed to do that in order to deliver myself out of an irritating situation of social bondage. Actually the thought of a spirit sneaking in to guzzle wine right at the table where you sat was the only part of the service that frightened Charles. "I want to see the ghost but I don't," he kept whispering to me. Little did he know that he was looking at her, two goblets drained and more coming. Little did he know that he was being introduced to one of life's most common refrains. *I want to know the truth but I don't.* It's the substance of the Garden of Eden and Pandora's box and every crime that takes place on your street.

THE DOWNSIDE IN incorporating knowledge and an open mind and respect for all religions in young children is the blurring of facts. Though I see a kind of sweetness in Easter bunnies hiding matzo and Santa lighting menorahs and fat Buddha statues draped in rosaries, there are also times when I desire absolute clarity. This is good and this is not. Here is a beginning and here is the end. Black/white. Frozen/thawed. Oral/anal. Major problem worth more money than you can earn in a lifetime or little do-it-yourself Home Depot job.

I sniff the air and would not be surprised to find that herd of dead horses piled up in my yard. Panic sets in. A chill that I have not felt since waking alone the day after Clark moved out. I knew even then, legs stretched out onto that cool empty side of the bed, that the fear I was feeling was not about what was behind me or regret over where I was but about moving forward on my own, no one there to share or even pretend to share the responsibility and burden of everyday mishaps and mistakes. There was no far off promise of the sort people make when trying to patch something broken without looking at what caused the damage—the anniversary surprise, the family vacation, the addition to the house that might take years to complete—pretty pastel Band-Aids applied to a series of hemorrhages. This fear of nothingness is why many people stay put even when unhappy and disillusioned, daily sidestepping the problems and debris. It is why they ask the four questions again and again as they seek their own answer within. *No, but really, how are you?* Many choose comfort within the known boundaries—sticking with Old World order as opposed to striking out for new lands and possibly falling off the edge of the earth.

"You invited them for drinks?" My friend Gretchen comes immediately when I call to say I need help. She stands in my driveway in her terry cloth robe, coffee cup in hand, car door still standing open. She is stuck with the very beginning part of my story and thinks this is the tragedy at hand. "What kind of drink, arsenic?" She steps close, invading my space, so I look away, into her backseat, where I see piles of what is probably much of Santa Claus for her three kids. "Have you lost your mind?"

"You don't have time for this," I say and point to the septic area, but she continues pressing, her hand heavy on my shoulder. "I don't know why I invited them except he's probably going to marry her and I want her to be nice to my children." I twist away and for the first time she takes in the stench.

"My God, what died?"

"Jesus," Charles says from behind me, the little nativity figures all gathered in his hand. "Jesus died for your sins."

"Well, I'm glad somebody did," Gretchen says, and she finally listens to what is the real problem. She suggests that the first thing I do is call and cancel the drop by and then go to the Yellow Pages and start begging. "Cry if you can," she says. "Play the divorce card. Single mom, young kids. Christmas Eve. Come to my house. Get a motel."

"And Hanukkah," Charles adds. "And Kwanzaa and the New Year parade. Passover is like Easter."

"You are all confused," Gretchen says and shakes her head. She squeezes my shoulder to emphasize the point and I nod along with her, making eye contact that she can't afford to hold too long. She has asked all the questions and more; she has even confessed her envy of my situation on numerous occasions and then, like most, immediately retreated back into the unspoken realm of financial security, where every minute of the day is absorbed into a defined journey marked by shimmering promises that may or may not come to pass. She catches my glance to her backseat, filled I see now with bags from FAO Schwarz, Neiman Marcus, and Bloomingdale's, and looks embarrassed.

"Don't look, your present is in there," and then she pulls me back into my house and opens the Yellow Pages on my kitchen table, a table I have carried around with me for over twenty years now, a table that once stood in my childhood kitchen and now is held together by coats of paint, many of which I applied myself over the years. "Here. Just start at the top and work down. Chances are we're not going to get anybody to come today but maybe Chad knows someone who can help us."

"The man always knows," I say, attempting a light laugh, but it sounds sarcastic and edgy even to my own ear. "Sorry, I didn't mean it that way."

"Well, I didn't mean it that way," she says. "Really I didn't."

I should tell her how often I have gone to the phone in recent years to call my father for the missing answer only to remember halfway through dialing that he is no longer there. It was one of the horses flogged early in the marriage. *You go running home for everything.* Wouldn't need to if I weren't alone. *You're an adult, handle it.* You handle it. *I work for a living.* So do I. And then it quickly spiraled until somebody got tired or too hurt or a child came in.

Now she hands me the phone. "Dial. I'll stay until something happens."

I close my eyes and wave one finger around in the air and then zoom in and land on the page. Settle Septic Systems. I get a recording as I assumed I would, try to sound as desperate as I feel. I am about to dial the next one—Pete's Power Pump. (What is it with all the alliteration?) Pete's slogan is WE SUCK. I am debating going with this one but fearful about who might show up—porn-star wannabe or someone content and proud to do poor work. Before I can even dial, the phone rings, and I answer to find Mr. M. Morris Settle himself, who says that normally he doesn't work on Christmas Eve but just happened to hear my message while in his office looking for pliers to tighten their tree stand. "Bad luck to have a tree fall," he says. "Mine fell one year and everything in my life changed afterward." He laughs and I hear drawers opening and closing, Christmas music playing in the background.

"You sound a little beside yourself," he says, and I assure him that yes, I am. I am completely beside myself, any more so and I'd be a town over from myself. And then within minutes, when I give him the address, he is on the case—knows the house, pumped it ten years ago and can tell me all about who lived here and their septic habits if I'm interested in hearing. They were wasteful people, kept trying to flush things that were bad for the system. "A lot of people think if it leaves the bowl then everything's hunky-dory, right? Out of sight, out of mind," he says and then keeps going before I can ask when he can come. "It's a complicated journey from beginning to end. It's like life that way." He puts down the phone and yells that he'll be right there. Brenda Lee is singing "Rockin' Around the Christmas Tree."

"He's coming," I finally announce, but everyone except Beau has moved on. I hear Gretchen ask the boys what they want Santa to bring and I purposefully do not listen for fear they have changed their minds again and my own stash in the attic, aside from being quite a bit more modest than they've ever encountered, will also be outdated.

I REACH UNDER the kitchen table, as I often do, to feel the thick painted letters of my own name. I was eight when I did that, thinking all the while that I would remember that moment forever. My parents didn't know I was under there, and I lifted the long tablecloth enough to see their feet rocking back and forth as they hugged there in the late afternoon light. He wore olive-colored Hush Puppies, perhaps why I was so drawn to Beau in the first place, and she wore pristine white Keds with little tassel socks, her legs tan and muscular—young. My dad had just gotten a new job and they were filled with ideas and promises about the future—a bigger house, she wouldn't have to work so hard, a real vacation. I would one day go to college. They would live to be very old so they could enjoy all the rewards of life. I listened and quietly painted my name with thick old paint, almost pastelike, as I went over and over each letter to ensure my existence and the permanence of the moment. My pulse raced with their joy and anticipation. What I wanted then was an Easy-Bake oven, a sibling, and a dog. But mostly I just wanted it all to last, this heady anticipation.

FOR MOST OF MY MARRIAGE, I felt all shook up like a can of paint in the hardware store. Activities and projects—one day bleeding into the next. Any average day, I was scattered to and fro—a Jackson Pollock canvas, and if there was any rhyme or reason, I couldn't see beyond the surface color and pattern. Lose your calendar or dare to admit the truth and the world might suddenly stop. But then the world does stop. You need for it to stop. One day you are shaking and planning, thinking how all you really need is a fresh coat of paint on everything, a whitewash of denial to make it all clean and new and perfect for starting over, and then the next day you lose all traction and have no choice but to call time. *I'm tired. I quit. I can't do this anymore.* The world stops and the dust settles and there is clarity. The heavy pigment sinks and the oil gathers on the surface, and like a can long abandoned, you can shake until the cows come home but the two will never blend again.

The disagreements. The grievances. They aren't sudden. They sound so trite and yet there they are. Irreconcilable differences.

I envy the people with something big to tell. How wonderful it would be to say: *Yes, I walked in on him having sex with the babysitter. That is what made THAT night different from all others. Yes, he had a cocaine habit and snorted up all the money for college. He beat me and I had two broken arms and now wear dentures.* Black and white. Dead or alive. Instead you say, *We're just too different, too far apart.*

Now I watch Gretchen driving away with the promise that she will check on me later, that, if needed, she will definitely call and cancel the evening on my behalf. Mr. M. Morris Settle will be here any minute. He said he first needed to run to the store for apple cider. I'm watching the window while sitting at my kitchen table with a pile of Christmas paper and ribbons, wrapping things that are easily adaptable for the exes should someone hand me a gift: nice bottle of wine, soaps, tea towels, chocolates. Charles is standing there watching me, that glass of chocolate milk still in his hand. He keeps dipping a finger in and dousing out the plagues—clearly the highlight of any Passover Seder. "Toads and boils and blood and lice." He waits for me to screech and say, "Ooh, yuk."

"Scabs and poop." He douses again and I can't help but laugh.

"Ooh, scabs and crap," I say, and his eyes widen in delight. "Snot and pee and pus and vomit." He screams with laughter and then runs off to tell his brother.

Mr. M. Morris Settle is tall and lanky with a shock of white hair he repeatedly smoothes back in a way that has left little flips like wings over each ear. He doesn't look like someone dressed for this kind of work. He's in khakis with crisp pressed pleats, a white dress shirt, and a bright green and red bolo.

He introduces himself with a firm handshake and then stands, hands on his hips as he tilts back his head and sniffs the air. "Oh yeah," he says. "We're smelling something all right." He looks at me and winks. "But I've smelled worse, honey. I sure have smelled worse."

"Thanks for coming on such short notice." Without warning my eyes fill with tears, and it makes me furious, like when I cry over a long-distance commercial or some movie designed to yank my chain. "I . . ." I reach my hands up, stalling so I don't cry, floundering for words.

"And that's just why I'm here," he says. "No need to say a word. If my Edie called anybody sounding that way, I'd like to think she'd get everything she needed just like that," he snaps his fingers and reaches in the passenger side of his truck for a crowbar. The truck is enormous with a huge tube snaked around the back. "No sir, I do believe you reap what you sow." He goes over to the rectangle of grass, steps hard with one foot as he feels around. Then he starts sinking the crow bar until there is a clanking sound. He whistles the whole while he goes back and forth—"Have Yourself a Merry Little Christmas," "Joy to the World." He pulls some big rubber boots over his dress shoes and starts carefully digging away the grass and setting it off to the side.

"Folks say I can come and go out of a yard and they don't even know I've been there." He reaches and pulls off the grate and sets it aside. "Nice work. Don't see a thing wrong down here." He calls me over and I squat there beside him as we peer down into the tomblike hole, brown sludge at the bottom.

"Beautiful sight in my line of work," he says and laughs. "The eye of the beholder. Yeah, you got a fine system. Redone since I was last here. Ain't even necessary to pump but I will and then we'll have a schedule."

"But the smell."

"That's a case of being in the wrong place at the wrong time." He shields his eyes and points at a squat silver cap on my roof. "Is that a bathroom right there?"

I nod, immediately picturing the bathroom I had all but lifted from the other house, the walls painted a bright blue like a pool, and big shiny goldfish on the shower curtain. I had lifted their bedrooms as well, attempting to make the transition as easy as possible, posters placed the same distance from the bed so that when they settled in at night there was the comfort of what they knew and recognized. SpongeBob SquarePants and World Wrestling Entertainment.

"You ever been in the wrong place at the wrong time?" he asks.

"Oh yeah."

"Well, that's your vent, and when your heat comes on in the house, then the air in all the vents is fighting to get out." He does his hands up and down and back and forth as if in battle. "Gotta go somewhere—and if you're standing here, and the wind is blowing just right over your roof and near that vent, poof, there you go."

"Wrong place at the wrong time," I echo.

"Story of my life." He looks at me and smiles, lines wrinkling around his eyes. "Or was. Before Edie. I'd jump down there and swim in that mess if I needed to for her. Anything at all, I'd do it." He pauses to make sure I'm listening. "I did *not* feel that way about Pamela." He doesn't even give me a chance to ask who Pamela is. "First wife," he whispers, as if she is somewhere nearby. "Left me right after that Christmas the tree fell. Never thought I'd be divorced and then I was. Grown kids. House paid off. I'm looking to retirement and the golden years and then boom." He stares, blue eyes fixed on mine in a way that makes it impossible to look elsewhere. There are bells on his bolo and he jingles when he shakes his head to emphasize his disbelief of his experience. His initials are embroidered on the pocket of his shirt and he wears a button that says BELIEVE. *In what?* I want to ask, but he continues without missing a beat. "I felt bad like I done wrong and I told people I felt I'd done wrong and friends finally said, Morris, that woman will never be satisfied. You did as much as a human could do. You did more than most humans would do, trying to make her feel happy, but the truth is you can't take a miserable person and turn them happy so you ought to be glad she went on and left you. It's a blessing, a gift. Flush her, man." He laughs. "That's what this one friend of mine says to me over and over—"flush her, man"—he's got a good sense of humor about my business, always has, like he's always saying to me at a card game—or used to say, since now that I got Edie I don't like late nights out playing cards, and those fellas can't stand that, can't stand I'm so happy—but he used to always say, 'A flush beats a full house don't it, Morris?'" He waits as if to let me catch up on his story, but then I realize he's still mulling over my system, shining his light from one dark corner to the next. "Run in there and give her a flush."

"Now? The one upstairs?"

"Yeah sure. Let's just add some gravy to the stew." I stand and nod. "Yeah, they all said it was a blessing, but I couldn't listen real good at the time. Part of it was I was thinking, *If it's such a blessing, why didn't somebody tell me how bad it was?* I was unhappy and didn't even know how much. You get used to the bad and don't know what you're missing. Like if you got used to the smell there you'd start to forget what smells good in this world. I can fix that with a length of pole, easy job. My kids took it better than I did. They weren't surprised either, and I said, *Well hell, what kind of idiot am I? Why couldn't I see what everybody else was seeing so easy?*"

I pause at the door to wait for him to finish. I can hear the television going full blast in the other room. I can see chocolate milk and Cocoa Puffs all over the kitchen counter.

"Go on, now," he motions. "Go flush, and when you get back I'll tell you about those trashy people who used to live here."

"I just got divorced," I say and step in before he can respond. I hear the heat come on and imagine a cloud of air traveling through the pipes up to the roof and open sky. I pass through the small family room, where Charles is about to doze off with his head on Beau's back. Michael is drawing cars, page after page of cars, while watching cartoons and making racing noises. Upstairs I tiptoe as if it is night and they are both in bed sleeping, as if I am viewing my life from some distant place. I can see Mr. Settle still squatting by the opening. I can tell he's still singing, hands patting his thighs. He looks up at the window and smiles though I know he can't see me there through the tilted blinds. I flush and then hurry back down, suddenly interested in what happens at the other end as well as hearing the rest of his story, eager to reenter my life.

"Perfect," he says and motions for me to squat there beside him again. "That smell ain't new. You just noticed it is all. I'll get you a length of pipe and swing by after the holidays, then it'll be high enough to blow away, just the birds will smell it." I nod, mesmerized by his voice and the swirl of brown water down below. "Still, let's pump it out—pump out the old and bring in the new."

"There you go now," he says when I laugh, and he starts unwrapping the big hose and pulls it over to the hole. "I believe there's nothing like a good hard laugh." Within minutes that tube springs to life, a motor grinding as it sucks the very crap from my life, and he has to talk even louder. "You know, in my line of work you're reminded that there's always crap to deal with. I think folks who don't deal with a little crap at a time forget how, and then they get hit with something big and fall to pieces. A little crap is good for you; it's like bacteria down there in your septic or, you know, in a fish tank or your innards. That's my two cents. Chicken soup for the outhouse set." He laughs and untwists a kink in the big hose. "I felt like such a failure back then." He shakes his head. "I was hittin' the sauce pretty hard, sitting and staring into pit after pit like this and thinking, *what a pile of shit*—pardon my French—but then you know what happened?"

"Edie?"

"Ah yeah, Edie—this world's best and most beautiful natural air freshener. I went to play bridge one night and there she was. Neither of us like bridge much—too much thinking so it messes up the talking. The fella having the gathering finally said, 'Why don't you two chatty boxes just go on and leave since you ain't paying attention to anybody else or the game anyway.' I don't even know what all we talked about, just that I hadn't talked and laughed like that in ages. We went to get us some coffee—we both love our coffee—and she told me that she liked hearing me sing. I guess I'd hummed a little here and there and didn't even know it. Maybe nervous, you know?"

I nod.

"Know why that was a kind of beautiful thing?" he waits until I shake my head. "I can't sing a note. Couldn't sing my way out of a paper sack and here's this sweet good-looking gal asking for more. Six years since I met Edie. I am seventy-three years old and these have been the best six years of my life." He leans in close, our shoulders touching as we both continue to stare down—the water level has dropped considerably. "Your life is just beginning," he nudges me, his arm firm against my own. "You're still wet behind the ears." He smells like cedar and Old Spice, and I catch myself with a quick image of him and Edie waking and preparing for this day. Their Christmas tree in its stand, coffee perking, bathroom mirror still steamed over as he ties his bolo and promises to be right back. "Dealing with all this crap right now will make everything better and brighter on down the road."

I wait, unable to look up, even though I know he's staring at me. He puts his hand on my back and rests it there a long comfortable minute and then he is up and moving. Edie is waiting, he says. They have stuff to do before the grandkids arrive; they like to go caroling with a group from the neighborhood—he drives his smaller truck, which doesn't smell like the business, and folks sit there in the back on hay and blankets; Edie sits back there a little bit, but mostly she likes to be there beside him. Then before bed, he and Edie like to sit by the fire and talk. "We both like to talk," he laughs. "Edie can outtalk me on a good day but I can hold my own. I know that's hard to believe but I can." He pulls and recoils the huge tube. "You're fine," he says and points to the rectangle of brown grass that looks just as it did when he arrived. "I believe everything's fine. Make sure your tree's in there tight. I wire mine up to the ceiling. Ain't taking any chances on Edie." And then he is gone, all the debris of my life sucked away and hauled off in his big silver truck and I am left wondering if he was even for real. When Gretchen calls to get the report, I tell her all about this incredible visit, how I feel the best I have felt in years. I feel alive, hopeful. I want to say that I feel I've been visited by an angel, that whoever is in charge of the great beyond would know that I would never believe in white gowns and shiny wings. My angel would never play a harp and sing sweetly on high; no, my angel vacuums crap and bad odors and worries. My angel talks too much and thrives on bad jokes. "He didn't even bill me," I say, further proof of the wonder of it all.

"He knows where you live," she says, desperate to turn the conversation back to what I plan to wear, cook, say at this ridiculous event I've planned. "He'll bill you." And I am thinking the bill will make it even better, as well as his return to install the pipe to vent leftover bad air when a rush of warmth blows from the furnace. I will love nothing better than to have that vent firmly in place and to know that he is real.

So, WHAT MAKES this night different from all other nights?

My tree is wired to a big sturdy hook in the ceiling and Christmas music is playing from three different sources. Clark's girlfriend has TMJ problems and carpal tunnel syndrome. I have to avoid looking at the boys when she first walks in with little wrist braces and a tight jaw. She, like Clark, is allergic to Beau and to the Christmas tree and to the dust mites. My ex-in-laws are cordial and like their soaps and chocolates. It is a little awkward and formal. It is easier when we all just focus on the boys and listen as they tell what they hope Santa Claus will bring. They have tied felt antlers to Beau's head and he sits looking at me with those big sad eyes as if pleading for my intervention. We both are eager for the visit to end. When Beau rolls over and quits participating, I fill the silence by saying I like my acrylic cookbook holder that keeps food from splashing on the pages, which is a lie. I told him years ago that I didn't need or want one of these, that I like how my favorite recipes are coated with necessary ingredients. Challah recipe glazed in dried dough and loose poppy seeds, cranberry bread with red smudges, Russian rye with a sticky molasses corner and little caraway seeds. "Thank you very much," I say with the practiced clear speech of a ventriloquist, because those words didn't come from me but from some person far across the years who dreams of clear fresh water just up ahead on the horizon. Yet, I am here, in my own house, awash with everything new. I am so dipped and bathed and resurrected that I expect to find a puddle on the floor around me.

When it is time for good-byes and I walk them to the door, Clark tilts his head to the breeze and comments that something must be wrong with the sewer system. "You need to get that checked," he whispers, while Nanci goes to the bathroom.

I smile and say thank you without moving my lips. Now Charles has his brother dousing plagues as well, even though their grandmother keeps pointing out that they are in the wrong holiday. I can tell she wants me to make them stop. "Blood. Guts. Puke." They fall out laughing and I ignore all the looks. I call out cheerful good-byes and happy holidays. Then I focus on the nativity scene, where Mary pulls her coat close around her and stares up into the dark night sky. Joseph has driven away in his little green car, and now it is once again just the three of them. She breathes deeply. Behind her, within the warmth of the manger, Jesus and Spiderman are happily talking and laughing. They are swaddled in worn soft quilts while they drink eggnog and rid the world of plagues and pestilence. She ponders this in her heart and it is good. There is no place on earth she would rather be. And that is what makes this night different from all the rest.

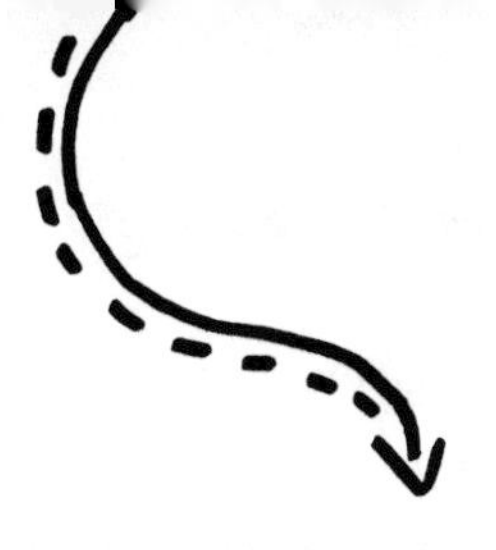

ANOTHER DIMENSION

Ann has not been back to her childhood home in over two years, not since the death of her father, but her brother, Jimmy, has updated her on all the changes he and his new wife have made. Ann has not met the new wife but could tell from the pictures Jimmy sent at Christmas that she looks a lot like the ones before her: short, blond, young, some pedigree or another Jimmy will find worth telling. Ann's luck with lasting relationships has been just as bad as his, the difference being she hasn't married all of hers. "That's because I'm honorable," he said during his last divorce when she pointed this out. "Or stupid," she responded, falling into the sarcastic sparring that had long ago become their way of communicating. Her first and only wedding ring was then in place on a finger she hoped might some day plump around it, claiming permanence, as she'd once admired on an older neighbor who, after forty years, couldn't get hers over her knuckle. The trapped ring reminded Ann of a photograph she once saw, a tree grown around and embracing a tombstone, both recognizable for what they were and yet now joined and inseparable in the most natural way. But now she is returning, post-divorce, to collect Jimmy's *I told you so* in person or maybe to see if she *can* return. Call it tired of running. Call it an exorcism.

RIGHT AFTER THEIR mother's death, when Ann and Jimmy were kids, their dad had dated somewhat indiscriminately. Therapists might have suggested he do things differently but he *was* a therapist and assumed he knew best. "Besides," he said at the end of his life, hospice care and their stoic stepmother and her polished professional children in the kitchen planning the details of his funeral as well as her move to a condo in Atlanta, "your mother was dying for so long. Did anyone ever look at it from my point of view?" He was a frail abbreviated version of himself by then and yet he talked more in those last days than he had ever talked. Still, there was much left unsaid.

THEIR DAD WAS a reasonably nice-looking man, and when their mother died, he was only forty-three, five years younger than Ann is now. Jimmy had manifested his looks, the long lean legs and nonexistent ass, which looked fine on a young guy in Levi's but kind of pitiful on a grown man. Still, their father had a head full of thick gray hair he kept cut close and he kept himself fit by nightly sit-ups and walking the golf course from sunup to sundown every Saturday and Sunday that he could. If there was anything that appeared unattractive about him, it certainly didn't stop the calls and indications of interest—things he said began happening the year *before* their mother died, when Jimmy was in fourth grade and Ann was in first. He never revealed their names but it left Ann with a sense of distrust for many of those who arrived with arms full of food and sympathy and, later in her life, of those who wanted to hover too close and comfort her during a difficult relationship. When their dad headed out on a date, Jimmy said things like: *At least pick one with a vertebra and opposable thumbs. One not beaten up by the ugly stick. One who won't steal Mom's things.*

Their mother was the real beauty of the family, or so everyone said, and she had grown more and more beautiful in these decades since her death, forever preserved in the family portrait that had hung in their dad's waiting room, where depressed and troubled people had to sit and look at the perfect image of a perfect family. Autumn day—Pongo Lake—idyllic picnic spread: a wicker hamper draped in antique linen, bone china plate with deep-purple grapes and a thick crust of bread. Ann has often imagined the scene, striving to recall every little detail, as if studying one of those hidden pictures, looking for the missing piece, the explanation that must be housed there, the bit of insight that has the power to pull her whole childhood together with a secure snap so that she might move forward once and for all. All that she has pulled from memory, though, is that when she lifted the basket lid, it was empty. And when she bit into one of the grapes, it was soft and rubbery, part of the artificial fruit that graced the milk-glass bowl always centered on the mahogany sideboard of their dining room. When she said she was hungry her mother said they were just there for the photograph and promised they would stop somewhere on the way home. Ann begged for the E&R Drive-In, a place famous for foot-long hotdogs and the little order boxes like parking meters at each spot. But she can't remember if they stopped or drove straight home. She can't remember what happened beyond sitting there in itchy church clothes, her mother's thin cool fingers pressing Ann's leg to keep her from jiggling, and an affected man in tight black clothing posing them like mannequins and then insisting they relax and look natural and happily joyful on this exquisite and delicious family outing.

Their dad had a few sleepovers in those early years. He thought he was being discreet but it would have been hard to miss the parade of women tiptoeing to the front door between midnight and dawn, traces of their fragrances lingering behind, on the living room sofa and on their dad's bedspread, the one their mother had custom made complete with shams and window treatments because she hadn't been able to find exactly what she wanted in any of the stores. The women were probably only thirty or forty at the oldest, but in Ann's memory, they were all old, and they all ran together, dark, light, plump, thin like funhouse mirrors, only not fun at all. Their voices went all singsongy when they saw Ann, speaking to her the way people talk to babies and kittens, sweet and fake and sometimes with gritted teeth like they could just as easily squeeze her to death like a boa constrictor.

"Major dog fight," Jimmy often reported with a bark or a growl, Ann relying on his every thought and belief. "Hope she was fixed."

If either said anything about the women to their dad, he blinked in a way that was distant and dismissive, like a robot being charged before quickly shifting topics. "How's football?"

"Football sucks," Jimmy said. "And I hate school." Jimmy had been a star athlete in the Pony League, but nothing seemed to matter anymore.

"Well, it will improve."

"That's what you said about Mom two years ago," Jimmy started laughing then—nervous, loud laughter—and as always Ann joined in. It was true after all. Their dad had never been able to tell them the truth about how sick their mother was and instead they learned from a neighbor who wasn't even close to them but was aggressive and nosey enough to think she had the right to try and make them face reality. She said it was her Christian duty to share the truth, and she used words like *incurable, terminal,* and *heaven*, her breath sharp with the spearmint gum clenched in her teeth. Then with a loud burdened sigh and sympathetic smile, she patted their backs and handed off a long rock-hard loaf of French bread, which Jimmy later used for a Wiffle ball bat.

Back when their mother was sick in her darkened room, they were obsessed with scary stories and movies. There was not enough manufactured fear in the world to erase the pain and sense of dread that filled their own house, but it was a way of forgetting, if only briefly. They rose early on Saturday mornings for Shock Theatre, imitating lines from *The Fly*—*help me, help me*—or walking like Frankenstein's monster. Jimmy liked to shine a flashlight under his chin, lower jaw thrust forward like a skeleton, or pull his buttoned shirt all the way up so he looked headless. They loved *Hush . . . Hush, Sweet Charlotte* and *Whatever Happened to Baby Jane?* and they scoured the *TV Guide* for any mention of Hitchcock's *Psycho* or *The Birds*. They liked the reruns of his television show, too, but their favorite show of all was *The Twilight Zone*, and in between times when they actually got to watch, they entertained themselves by recounting the episodes that scared them the most: a goblin on the wing of a plane making a man go nuts, and the Talking Tina doll that murders Telly Savalas, and the little girl who goes under her bed and rolls through an invisible hole into another dimension. That episode reinforced every fear Ann already had, darkness, being lost, the maniac-under-the-bed story Jimmy liked to tell, the one where the girl keeps putting her hand down for her dog to lick her because if her dog licks her then everything is okay. But of course, everything was not okay and in the morning the dog was dead and there was a note that said, "Maniacs can lick, too." It was so horrible that, when she thought of it, she forgot the way her mother looked there in the other room, the way she could barely lift a hand to touch Ann's face, the way the room smelled heavy and overripe with bad things to come.

Ann had to leap in and out of bed for years because of the maniac and the other dimension, and even as an adult, when making the bed, she is still aware of how vulnerable her feet look there at the edge of darkness beyond the dust ruffle and spread. Sometimes she can't help but fall to her hands and knees and look, to see whatever is lurking there before it sees her.

"What will you do if you find something?" her husband had asked a year into their marriage. The question surprised her. She had not even been aware of looking, and yet there she was crouched on all fours and peering into the dusty darkness, looking for the invisible hole where she might disappear, so aware that she was already looking for a way out, that the loose ring on her finger had not made her feel safe and connected at all. If anything, it had left her shocked and numbed by how conditional her life felt.

• • •

Going Away Shoes

NOT LONG AFTER their mother died, Ann and Jimmy saw a *Twilight Zone* episode where children who have lost their mother are able to pick parts to create a robotic grandmother: the eyes, the hands, the voice. It was hard to watch because the girl's name was the same as her own, so she distracted herself by the reality beyond the show, how really the girl was Angela Cartwright, known best for getting to be a kid in *The Sound of Music* and the younger daughter on *Lost in Space*. "And look," she told Jimmy, "the dad is really Larry Tate from *Bewitched*." But Jimmy started crying when they were sifting through what looked like marbles, picking the right eyes, searching for those most loving and motherly. He screamed at the television that he couldn't remember her eyes anymore, that he sometimes couldn't remember her face or her voice, and then got furious, threatening to beat the shit out of Ann if she ever told she'd seen him cry.

WHEN JIMMY WAS in the sixth grade and Ann in the third, there was one woman their dad really liked being with. She was nothing like their mother and nothing like all the others they'd seen in what Jimmy called the "Country Club Dog Parade." The woman was average looking, little to no makeup, frizzy dark hair yanked back in a loose ponytail, and a silver ankh around her neck. Her car was littered with thrift-shop finds and good grocery store deals. She was always appearing with things just out of style or not the real thing that she gave freely to kids who came into the restaurant where she worked: Babette instead of Barbie, Soldier Jim instead of G.I. Joe. She always had bags of rings like you might get at the dentist office or in a gum machine, wax lips and those little wax bottles filled with sugar water. They called her "Dime Store Dodo" and then "Rosemary Looney" because she was always playing her records and singing along, "Hey there, you with the stars in your eyes," when she came over to cook dinner, which got to be more and more often. She even did the little talking parts of the song when she thought she was all alone and staring at herself in the chrome of the toaster or the reflection in the kitchen window. She loved Doris Day, too, so Jimmy often mimicked a falsetto "Que Sera Sera" while answering the questions: "Will I be pretty?" *Hell no.* "Will I be rich?" *Only at Pine Cone Manor* (which was the county home for the poor over beside the Methodist church). He said she was Doris Day on the darkest night of her life, and though Ann laughed and went along with him, the truth was she had started looking forward to seeing Rosemary Looney and hearing her corny songs echoing through the house, smelling the familiar scent of her coat by the door like bread just baked or fried chicken. Ann practiced how to look like she was feeling nothing at all so Jimmy wouldn't read her thoughts and get angry at her.

Rosemary worked at a restaurant downtown known for calabash seafood and hush puppies, which is where their dad said he met her, though Jimmy insisted late one night that really

Rosemary Looney was one of their dad's patients and he'd gotten her from the state hospital the same way they'd gotten Bingo, an unruly beagle mix, from the pound. They still told their scary stories late at night, but it was getting harder and harder for Ann to listen; the images stayed with her longer now and kept her awake. Now that she could no longer wander into the room beside hers and find her mother still breathing there, it was hard to calm away the scary parts. She tried to picture her mother other ways, but like Jimmy, she found it getting harder and harder, and instead what she saw when she closed her eyes was what was left of her mother's body closed in the dark coffin. And Jimmy wasn't always there anymore. He got phone calls and closed his bedroom door. He spent more and more time with his friends. She wanted to think of funny stories, happy stories, but she didn't dare tell Jimmy for fear that he wouldn't spend any time at all with her. She just listened to his whispered stories and held tight to Bingo's collar so he wouldn't jump off and venture under the bed.

"We bonded over a FryDaddy," Rosemary liked to tell. "Your dad is such a healthy eater otherwise, so I felt like the devil of temptation. And I wondered, did he come to see me or did he come to eat deep-fried sweet batter?" She put a hot ceramic crock of chili on the table and then did a funny little dance, moving her hips and pointing to the chili like she had magically made it appear. She was wearing a T-shirt that said, I CAN'T BELIEVE I ATE

THE WHOLE THING, like the Alka-Seltzer commercial. Their dad grabbed Rosemary's hand and did a little dance himself, looking like an offbeat turkey in corduroy, and Ann felt both embarrassed and thrilled, like the time she dove into the lake and her suit bottom slid right off her ankles. It made her want to jump up and dance with them, beside and between, *with*, but Jimmy gave her a look that let her know that was not a good idea.

Their dad laughed at everything Rosemary Looney said and did. He laughed in a way that they had never even heard and that they didn't hear again in all the years left of his life once she was gone.

ROSEMARY LOONEY SEWED the letters of Jimmy's name on the back of his junior high football uniform and hemmed and fixed Ann's dance costumes, attaching the golden leaves to her leotard when she was a magic tree and adjusting her Polichinelle clown suit for *The Nutcracker*. Rosemary went to all three performances and then delighted in Ann's tales about how bad it smelled up under Big Mother Ginger's skirt—feet and butt smells—and on top of that Mother Ginger was a man. Rosemary said that Mother Ginger ate at the restaurant all the time and that he didn't smell good then, either, not even that one time he asked her for a date. Rosemary held her nose and crossed her eyes as she told it, then leaned forward and whispered in Ann's ear, "I told him I have a boyfriend." The words, the secret, Rosemary's warm hand on her cheek made Ann's chest pound with the fast beat of the music on the stereo and filled her with a giddiness that left her no choice but to run and jump on the sofa, then from chair to chair, singing along with Rosemary at the top of her lungs, "Come on-a my house, my house, I'm gonna give you everything."

Rosemary had a youthful face when you got right up close, something Ann liked to do more and more often. Rosemary's eyes often teared up in laughter when Ann told her what had happened at school or some corny joke—*Do your feet smell? Does your nose run? You're built upside down!* Rosemary knew lots of jokes like that from her own son. He was already in college, which she said was the reason she worked as many hours as she did. That and because she loved to cook. "You know," she told Ann one day after showing a photo of the boy—shoulder-length curly hair and love beads—"I was way too young to have a baby when I did, not but sixteen, but I wouldn't take anything under the sun for him. Best thing I ever did."

Ann wanted to love her, but Jimmy was determined to break it up. He told Rosemary how their mom had made a threat against any woman who ever tried to take her place. "It's a curse," he said. "You can pass through but you can't stay."

"I don't believe in such," she said and glanced over at Ann, maybe in hopes of some help Ann wasn't able to give. She was having to concentrate hard to keep her face without a feeling. "I'm gonna ask your dad what he thinks."

"He doesn't know. Because see, the bad stuff will happen to him, so it's not like you'll get *your* head sliced off in a wreck or get shot. You'll just make it all happen to him." There had been a time when Jimmy was obsessed with Jayne Mansfield's death, the details of her decapitation in the car wreck. Jimmy had found many deaths far more horrific than their mother's slow skeletal disappearance to fixate on—heads severed but hearts still beating, a man conscious while lions ate his legs and arms, the man who woke up in a crocodile den surrounded by decomposing bodies and had a heart attack while trying to swim away. He knew of drownings and fires, falls from high buildings and elevator shafts, and slit throats. Jimmy had taken Ann through the big trailer up at Crown Shopping Center that housed the car Bonnie and Clyde were killed in. It cost a quarter a look, and they had looked twelve times, each time getting lost in the bullet holes and rusty-colored blood stains, the place where they said Bonnie's head lay when all the shooting was over. Ann had memorized much of that song "The Ballad of Bonnie and Clyde"—"People let me tell you they were the devil's children"—but after seeing the real blood it made her sick to think of them. Bonnie didn't look anything like Faye Dunaway and Clyde didn't favor Warren Beatty at all.

"At least Mom isn't all bloody," Jimmy had said. Ann tried to hold onto his arm but he wouldn't let her. Some of his friends had come along and there was a girl he liked waiting to go on the

Tilt-A-Whirl, which along with Bonnie and Clyde's car, a Ferris wheel, and a pony ring with three very old and tired ponies, constituted the whole carnival.

"Here are the signs to watch for," Jimmy told Rosemary and then listed things their dad had always done, mainly things that got on their mother's nerves. The way he studied and picked at his fingernails or jiggled a finger in his ear when he was nervous, the way he stroked his nose while thinking, the way sometimes you would talk to him and he wouldn't have heard a single word you said because—he always said—he was rethinking what someone else with a problem had said earlier in the day.

"I've seen all that," Rosemary said and laughed. "I actually like all that about him. Shows he's human."

"But he's cursed," Jimmy said. "And he'll die if you stay with him. He'll die *because* of you."

"He's human," she said, "and you really need to think about what you're saying before you say it." She didn't smile as she usually did. She knocked wood and crossed herself and then ran a nervous hand up and through her hair as Ann had seen her do the day their dad got a surprise visit from one of their mom's old friends, who was all dressed up and smelling like she was on her way to someplace fancy. Their dad's favorite kind of pie, a lemon chess, was cradled in her long thin arms and she handed it and some cut flowers to Rosemary like she was a maid and asked her to take care of them, maybe make a pot of coffee while she visited. She was one of those women with perfect posture and talked without moving her mouth much. Rosemary's face was as blotched red that day as it was while she stood there staring back at Jimmy like they were doing a blink contest. He stomped out and slammed the door and Ann waited a little too long before following. She didn't want to leave at all, Rosemary was looking at her, and the large mixing bowl of pound cake batter she'd promised Ann she could lick there on the counter. By the time Ann got outside where Jimmy was pounding a tennis ball up against the garage door, he was calling her *traitor, Judas, pussy,* and that same night he took her Chatty Cathy doll and pulled her head off, said she looked too much like Talking Tina and he was afraid she'd murder their father if Rosemary didn't do it first.

Ann cried and threatened to tell. She said it was just a stupid show like the stupid show that made him *cry* over an old woman put together like a robot. "It wasn't even real," she said, "but you cried like a little tiny baby." She knew as soon as she said it that she shouldn't have, and she immediately begged his forgiveness, begged him to please not be angry at her. He said he would forgive her if she did everything he told her to do, including ignore Rosemary Looney. So she did. The most frightening thing he made her do was to venture down into the basement to get the dog food. He let her get all the way down and then she heard the door shut and the lock click into place. "Jimmy?" she called with the click, but he didn't answer. Then he turned out the light.

She froze waiting for him to help her and then she panicked. She screamed his name but got no response and then all the images were there, the talking doll and the child lost through the watery wall and flocks of birds smothering and pecking people to death. She saw them carry her mother from the house, a big green bag zipped up on a stretcher. She wanted to see her one more time but all her mind could conjure was a skeleton. She was crying then, feeling her way up the dirty splintered steps to pound on the door, pulling on the knob and begging. She thought of her mother closed up in darkness and of the maniac under the bed stabbing Bingo and licking her hand. She pictured Bonnie's bloody body and the psycho man dressed up like his mother. She screamed until she couldn't breathe and then he pushed the door open and she lost her balance, bumping and tumbling down the rough steps, a crack of pain up her arm as she hit the concrete floor and rolled into a stack of old magazines and papers. Then the light was back on, everything grainy in the brightness, and Jimmy was beside her, already making light of it all, what a baby she was to think he'd leave her there, she was okay, it was a joke, just a joke. They stared in amazement at her bone piercing the pale skin of her forearm. At first it hurt too much to cry and Jimmy looked and sounded so far away, and then she was screaming. All she remembered was screaming and then Jimmy running for help. The next thing she remembered, Rosemary was there and had her in the car. Rosemary wasn't singing and she never even turned the radio on. She just kept telling Ann that it would be okay, everything would be okay.

All the way to the hospital, Jimmy told how Ann had gone into the basement even though he told her not to, that Ann told him to turn out the lights so she could pretend she was the girl in *The Twilight Zone* episode. Rosemary Looney looked over at Ann, eyebrows raised in question. Ann had confided her fear of the dark one night, weeks before, just the two of them in the car while her dad cleaned the windshield and checked the oil. Rosemary and her dad had a dinner date and at the last minute no choice but to take Ann with them because the sitter canceled. She remembered Rosemary saying, "That's okay. It'll be fine." And it felt so good there in the car with her, the Mobil sign glowing in the window of the small cinder-block service station. Ann stared at the winged horse while she told Rosemary how the stories and movies scared her more than they used to, how some nights she couldn't sleep at all for thinking about all the bad things that could happen. It made her cry to think of Bonnie and Clyde gone so wrong—"the devil's children"—their bodies twitching and flinching with bullet spray. "The basement is worst of all," she whispered. She told how it reminded her of a grave, her mother's grave, and what it must be like for her in the dark dampness. She watched the winged horse, gone filmy, hooves raised and pawing the air, and she felt Rosemary's hand on her own, warm and firm in its hold and squeeze. Rosemary didn't tell her that she was being silly or that there was nothing to be afraid of. She said, "Sometimes our fears are there to protect us." She said, "What we can't afford to let them do is cripple us." She told Ann it felt good to talk, that she had really missed her lately, and Ann just nodded and leaned in as close as she could, no need to hide the relief she was feeling. "I hope you'll always feel you can talk to me."

"Ann?" she asked. They were almost at the hospital and Ann could feel Jimmy's gaze on her. "You did that, honey? You wanted to be in the basement without the light on?"

"Trying to beat her fears away," Jimmy said. "So she won't be *crippled* by them." The word on his tongue was ugly and harsh and Ann was sorry she had told him about the night in the car with Rosemary. How when her dad got back in, the three of them laughed and sang "Aba Daba Honeymoon" and then went and got hotdogs at the E&R and then ice cream at the Dairy Queen. They even rode out to see where the new Holiday Inn was being built on the interstate. It was going to have a pool twice the size of Howard Johnson's, and Rosemary knew somebody who worked there and could get them in to swim. "We'll all go swimming, right?" Rosemary asked and her dad reached and touched Rosemary's cheek. He said, "Yes." His hand dropped to her neck and pulled her closer. He said, "We will *all* go swimming." Ann told Jimmy everything, because she wanted him to like Rosemary, too. He loved swimming and he loved hotdogs. There was no reason *not* to want Rosemary to be their new mother and stay forever. The robot grandmother had done that. She stayed until Larry Tate's children were all grown up and had learned how to love.

"I'm so sorry, honey," Rosemary kept saying as she pulled into the hospital lot. "It's going to be okay."

It was in the emergency room that something else happened. When Rosemary went to the pay phone to call their father, Jimmy allowed the doctor to think that someone might have done this *to* Ann. Locked her in the basement or grabbed and twisted her skinny white arm, pushed her down those dark stairs. Jimmy stammered and paced as he told how he came home to find his sister that way and that Rosemary was in the kitchen. He said he didn't know how to tell their dad, their dad would be so hurt. He acted afraid and stopped talking when Rosemary reentered the room. She was wearing what she called her "work clothes"—old dirty white Keds, gray sweatpants, one of their dad's old shirts with an ink stain on the pocket too bad for him to wear to work.

"What?" she asked. She was reaching for Ann when the young doctor asked her to wait at the door. "What is it?" she asked. Jimmy had told Ann in the brief second the doctor took a phone call to flinch and cry when she saw Rosemary. "She's the devil's child," he said. "The goblin, the maniac under the bed." And though Ann knew it wasn't true, she couldn't help but sob when she saw her. She couldn't look at Rosemary's face so she looked at her father's stained shirt instead and then at Rosemary's silver necklace against her flushed throat and chest. "It's Egyptian for life and water and all kinds of good things," she had said that same day they danced all around the living room, throwing pillows and accidentally breaking a vase. "It's kinda like a cross but a lot softer."

The doctor said he needed to speak to Rosemary alone. A young nurse with bright orange hair took Ann to be x-rayed and then stayed with her the whole time. Open fracture and a greenstick fracture. The orange-haired nurse kept talking, keeping Ann's face turned away from the doctor bending over her arm and giving explanations of it all. How the open break was a doozy, but of course would heal just fine. And little greensticks happened all the time to kids. "Get it? Like a green stick? A little twig? You can stop crying," the orange-haired girl said. "It really will get better."

"What were you doing, skydiving?" The doctor laughed and the orange-haired girl moved just enough that Ann couldn't see her and then he didn't say anything else except that he bet Ann had lots of friends who would be begging to sign the cast. By the time Ann was ready to leave, her dad was there waiting, one arm around Jimmy's shoulder with a promise of E&R hotdogs and whatever she wanted for dessert. She looked around for Rosemary but she had already left.

• • •

"ANYONE WHO NEEDS me gone this bad," Rosemary said, pausing to swallow and take a deep breath, "deserves it, I guess." She said this to the two of them when they got home from the hospital and found her in the dusk-lit kitchen, their father outside explaining to a neighbor what had happened. Her eyes were red and swollen. She had started wearing mascara not long after the fancy pie lady showed up, and now it was all smudged on her flushed cheeks. Her shoulders rounded as she opened the pantry without a sound to reclaim the big silver mixer she had left there, a gleaming promise of more cakes and bread and homemade pimento cheese. "I just hope you will tell your father the truth." She walked to the door without looking back at either of them.

Late that night, Jimmy made Ann swear never to tell. "It's a graveyard secret," he said. "It goes with us down into the ground and we never mention it again." He paused then, jaw clenched tight as he tried not to cry himself, the anger that always accompanied his weak moments there on the horizon. He had gone over the story of what happened so many times—*she locked you in the basement for punishment*—she was feeling confused. "If we do break the graveyard secret," he said and reached as he normally would to clench and twist her arm but stopped just shy of her cast, "then it's like saying you never loved Mom. It's like hating Mom. And she'll know. She's listening right now and something really bad will happen to Dad." Ann was crying then, half listening to him, half wanting to run into their father's room and beg him to never die. "Take the vow," he said, and then she did, heavy promise poured and sealed in a concrete vault. And they never discussed it again, not even the times Ann wanted to, like whenever she thought of the way their dad and Rosemary had looked at each other or the way their dad had laughed during that little bit of time, a way she has yet to find in her own life, though God knows she has tried. She wanted to say something before their dad remarried, to speak, and not hold her peace when the minister made the request, but she wasn't able. Later she put it off, ever distracted by her own struggle to find a friendship she could trust and believe in—the equivalent of stumbling along a dark corridor in search of a light—but it became a journey with its own momentum, a runaway train, incessant daily activities turning weeks to months and then years.

Still, she had thought of Rosemary Looney often, like anytime she saw George Clooney featured on the cover of a magazine or when the legendary singer died and Ann saw photos of her as a young woman, the same photos that had stared out from the albums *their* Rosemary brought into the house to play while she cooked. Sometimes one of the old melodies, "Hey There" or "In the Cool, Cool, Cool of the Evening," got stuck in her head for days on end. It had been easier to fight against memory when living in Oregon and then Chicago, far removed from the South, where she wouldn't stand a prayer of running into anything deep-fried in that sweet calabash batter or waking to the suffocating humidity she associated with her mother's illness. She could fill her mind with new foods and places and people in a way that blocked and scrambled everything that hurt, everything except an arm bone faithful as an obedient dog when it came to predicting damp weather.

THE DAY AFTER her father's funeral, Ann was desperate to get out of the house and away from the tension of her own marriage, alarmed by how even illness and death of a loved one could not buy a temporary reprieve from it all. She escaped by taking her five-year-old stepdaughter, Sally, to Chuck E. Cheese. Her marriage was over and yet she was dragging her feet for dread of losing Sally and the time she had with the child every other week. Sally was what kept Ann from feeling regret about the path her life had taken. And that was what was on her mind as she stood there beside a mechanical horse, the child bumping and laughing along, singing "Do Your Ears Hang Low" and begging Ann to sing along. She kept thinking of her dad's life and how the last twenty years had been spent with a woman so similar to Ann's mother that it was like on *Bewitched* when the new Darrin slipped right in and took the place of the old without making mention of how different his features were, the eyes, the voice. Her stepmother slept in their mother's bed, sat at their mother's vanity, even sat in the same chair in the TV room, the smaller "hers" version of their dad's recliner. One Christmas Ann had even been surprised to see her wearing a cashmere cardigan that had been their mother's, the scent of White Shoulders deeply woven into the fabric. It was hard not to study it for a lingering strand of hair, her own DNA tangled in the fibers. It was easier that way.

Ann was thinking of that last day with her dad and how there were so many things she had always wanted to ask, preparing herself to do so if only he woke up one more time. And when she looked up, she saw someone who looked just like Rosemary Looney across the pizza-strewn kid-littered room, sitting with a toddler at one of the Formica booths, her hair almost completely gray but worn the same way. Ann thought of how Rosemary often sat on the arm of her dad's chair, how they all laughed when her round bottom slid down into his lap and his arms quickly locked around and held her there. He said he was never ever going to let her go and continued holding tight even when she squirmed and laughed and said she needed to go check on dinner.

ANN NEVER KNEW exactly how the two ended it, only that it was never the same after she broke her arm. Then one night, Rosemary stopped by—not to stay, she stressed, when Jimmy opened the door—but to gather up the rest of her pots and pans. Their dad had spent many recent nights there with them, sometimes asking about their days and offering help with homework, but usually just settling in with whatever they were watching on television. That night, Ann wandered out onto the back porch and saw him follow Rosemary to her car, heard Rosemary say, "Please, Bill." Ann's father's name on her tongue sounded so personal and revealing, and he looked weak and helpless, like he might fade into nothing. "You *know* I would never do anything to hurt them," she said. There was a long pause and then a gasp between sobs, something so inhuman and demeaning in the moment, not unlike the memory Ann had of her mother's thin white legs struggling in attempt to raise herself onto a bedpan. "You know me. You know better."

"But I can't risk losing their trust," he said. "What choice do I have?"

Ann strained to hear her answer if there was one. And at the end of so many relationships, she has thought that if only she knew the answer, if only she knew what Rosemary thought, then she might know the secret to finding something honest and lasting.

AND NOW ANN is ringing the doorbell, standing where Rosemary stood and took a long shaky breath before leaving that last time, where Ann's mother had been many summer nights as she called them in to supper, no knowledge of the minute cancer cells coursing through her blood. The pink dogwood tree they planted when their mother died fills the side yard. And the sight of Jimmy is a shock, like seeing their dad. "Hey sis," he says. "Look at you." His face is the same, just older, and when he hugs her close he feels so much like their father that she wants to let go and collapse into the tears and worries of a frightened eight-year-old, but then his wife is there, so easily wound up and slipped into the role of the lady of the house. He has done it all before. Three other times in fact. The old wife and two kids and dogs are across town. The one before her childless and in San Francisco. The one before that is rarely even mentioned, a few months post-college, a mutual mistake that should have just been a summer living together. And here is the new wife and new guinea pig–looking dog and the baby two months from being born.

"Come on in," he says and steps back, the open door like a time machine, a portal she fears entering, but then everything seems so different, it's a relief. Gone is the pale green carpet and formal Queen Anne furniture their mother loved, gone is the big braided rug in the family room, a horrible place to fall asleep for the weaves and marks left indented in your face. Now the living room is pale pink, and big cream leather sofa parts—ottomans and such and glass-topped tables—fill the space. An enormous entertainment center fills one whole wall. The only reminder of the past is the old free-standing radiator where Ann often huddled on winter mornings, her knees pulled up under a worn flannel gown, as she waited for Jimmy to come down to watch Shock Theatre. They are about to remove it and tear through the wall to build a Florida room.

"Perfect for watching the scary movies," Ann says pointing at the big-screen television and all the equipment parts stacked on top of it.

"We hate scary," Kaycie says and simulates a shudder, diamond-weighted hand pressed to her chest. "We're such wimps."

"Since when?"

"Always," Kaycie says before Jimmy can speak. She says they've been watching *The Thorn Birds* on DVD, something she remembered watching as a little girl.

"Good old Dr. Kildare," Ann says, but Kaycie is too young to remember the star in another form. She is too young to know Jimmy in another form, too.

Ann takes her shoes off and Kaycie watches her every move on that white carpet. For a moment it is as if their mother is there in the room about to reprimand but too weak to do so.

"James?" Kaycie calls. "Can you come help me, honey?" He smiles at Ann with the promise of a glass of wine and follows his young wife into the kitchen. This wife is a clone of the one before her, just a decade younger, with Jimmy starring in the same old role. Is there a missing piece of machinery that could, like switching a train track, throw him off in a new and different direction? Ann has often thought they jinxed themselves when they sabotaged Rosemary Looney, that Jimmy's threat of a curse placed on their dad was actually placed on them.

"You know, Kaycie's dad owns a Volvo dealership," Jimmy says when he returns. "He was a judge, really powerful guy and very well known all over the state. Retired early and now he's all into safety features like kid locks and side-view mirrors that get rid of your blind spot. Kaycie's an only kid so you can imagine how excited about this kid they are."

"James?" Kaycie calls again from the kitchen but he pretends he doesn't hear and keeps talking about cars and what he drives and what model Kaycie drives and why.

"When did you start going by James?" Ann asks, her tongue lengthening the name to feign British royalty, and he shrugs, tells her she can still just call him "master." He had called himself Jim as soon as he went away to college but she had never heard anyone call him James, not even their parents or grandparents.

Ann looks around the room, everything perfectly arranged, coffee table art, house magazines fanned on the end table, candlesticks aligned on the mantle. "She's so neat!" she says, but he thinks she means hip, groovy, cool and smiles proudly.

"How's the divorce?" he asks.

"It sucks," she says, thinking she can hit a familiar chord with what had been *his* answer to adultlike questions for years. "Why didn't you tell me what it would cost? I might as well have taken everything I owned and poured kerosene on it and struck a match." She hears herself speaking to him as she does everyone who asks, focusing on the money and the greedy lawyers and everything stereotypical and cliché about divorce so as not to have to think about Sally and the ache she feels for what she will never have again, any damage or hurt she might have caused. She is too old to have a child of her own and has abandoned the one who didn't really need her anyway. She was the surplus mother, the extra, the stand-in. "You're like the stunt parent," her husband had said in the beginning, delighted at how easily Sally adjusted to her, the way she sometimes got mixed up and called her "mama." "I'll let you do all the dangerous parts—diapers, runny noses, head lice." There was a whole list they had created and laughed about. She would volunteer for things like troop leader and Disney movies and trips to the mall. She would handle acne and bras, buy the tampons, and answer questions about sex. Somehow in all the imagining, she was always thinking about Rosemary Looney; she wanted to be for Sally what Rosemary might have been for her.

"The lawyer spent all of my retirement on a weekend in Aruba," she says and lifts her glass for a refill. "He said, 'I spent all the money you'll earn over the next three years on cocaine and a down payment on my summer home.' "

"He didn't say that," Kaycie calls from the kitchen. "My daddy is a lawyer so be nice."

"He said it telepathically," Ann says. "I read his mind." Jimmy laughs, holds his hand up to his forehead like Johnny Carson as Carnac.

"Ben-Gay," he says and points at Ann, punches and pushes her shoulder until she asks the question: "Why didn't Mrs. Franklin have any kids?"

"Bible Belt."

"What holds up Oral Roberts's pants?"

"Crabgrass."

"What do crabs get high on?"

There was a time when they could do this for hours, the best of Carnac committed to memory from all those years their dad was determined to spend time with them and the best way he knew how was taking an interest in the television shows they liked. In the years between Rosemary Looney and their stepmother, the television was like the fourth family member, the dummy at the bridge table, focus of many conversations. There was also a time when Jimmy might have dropped the routine for just a minute and asked how she was *really* doing, if she needed anything, but it seems this is unlikely now, especially when Kaycie comes back into the room.

"What are you two talking about?" She grabs Jimmy's hand and presses it to her stomach. "Are you being silly again?"

"No. We're talking divorce, death, bankruptcy." Jimmy smiles at Ann, close to a flicker of familiar, but then Kaycie pats and shakes his shoulders with an "*Oh you.*"

"You know," she turns to Ann wide-eyed and serious, "you should always pay off your credit card the second you get it. And pay cash for things like cars."

"Really?" Ann says, working to keep her thoughts from her face, and in that moment realizing that too much of the house is the same—the light, the smell, the door to the room at the top of the stairs where her mother died, the door to the basement where she broke her arm. She tries to catch Jimmy's eye but he is looking elsewhere, not a trace of response or emotion. If only they could make a rearview mirror to correct the blind spot of privilege and denial.

"We have a friend who got in so much trouble, and I know James would have helped him, but I knew better." Kaycie sits moving his hand round and round her stomach, the baby barely a bump on her tiny frame. She has said at least three times that she feels *huge*. "You cannot afford to help people, especially those close to you."

"It was Sam Rowland," Jimmy says. "Man, talk about a guy getting taken to the cleaners. His wife screwed him to the wall."

"And he should have thought about that while screwing that stupid office assistant," Kaycie adds. "You need smarter friends, honey."

"Jimmy," Ann says. "He's your best friend—or was—for your whole life." She watches Kaycie flinch when she calls him Jimmy, as if the boy she never knew isn't allowed in this room. "Is he okay?"

"He made some really bad and stupid choices," Kaycie says.

"Who hasn't?" Ann asks.

"He'll be okay," Jimmy interrupts, and Ann realizes she wasn't even thinking of Sam in that moment. She was thinking of herself and of Jimmy. She was thinking of their dad. She was thinking of that summer Jimmy came to her needing money and she gave him all she had earned and saved waiting tables. She gave him over a thousand dollars that, for all she knew, went up his nose or to get some girl an abortion or just to have an easy month or so between semesters.

WHEN JIMMY HID under his bed after their mother died, Ann was determined to find and be with him, even if it meant rolling into and through the wall herself and getting lost there in the vacuum of another dimension. He knew she was afraid to crawl under the bed, which is exactly why he went there. Their mother was buried earlier that day, and there was a mountain of Tupperware and Pyrex in the kitchen, their dad exhausted but politely thanking a throng of people. *Yes, cancer is very cruel. Yes, she's in a better place. Yes, no more suffering.* Jimmy was crying and didn't want anyone to see him. He was angry.

"Please let me come." She begged. She clutched the leg of his blue jeans as she inched her body under there and waited for her eyes to adjust.

"No, get out of here." He kicked away from her and she began crying uncontrollably, overwhelmed by the darkness and the thought of being all alone.

"Do you remember that day at Pongo Lake?" she asks when Kaycie returns to the kitchen. "The day that creepy guy took our picture?"

"Of course. Why?" He holds his hand up to his forehead and threatens to start the game again but she interrupts him.

"There was nothing in the hamper," she says. "Mom wasn't even sick yet but there wasn't any food. It was all fake." It feels good to say it, to acknowledge what she has come to think in recent years. The sadness was already there, coating their lives like mildew, and then they allowed the illness to eclipse and camouflage everything. "I think they were never really happy."

"Sure they were."

"I don't think so."

"Well, I think so," he says. "At least until she got sick."

"No," Ann says. "The sickness just gave them a reason they were willing to admit. I bet if she had lived they would have divorced." Ann is on a roll now and has to finish. "Or worse, they would have lived together unhappily for the rest of their lives."

"Oh how ridiculous." Kaycie comes in and waves her hand dismissively. "You two were terrors. Who could have acted happy? And what you did later to run off that redneck fry cook!" She is laughing, her beautiful face animated by her amusement. "I mean you were right to do it, but still, it was so *mean*."

There is a crack of splintered silence, a struggle for balance, and then Jimmy moves on. She can tell that the impulse to tell a joke is alive on his tongue, but he goes the safer route and asks about her work as a high school guidance counselor, the same kinds of questions she gets asked by people meeting her for the first time: *Do kids come to you with personal problems? Is it all confidential? Do you help them prepare for tests?* Jimmy had spoken the words they vowed never to speak, words sworn on their parents' lives. Had he told all the wives? Confessed some late night to each the terrible thing he and his little sister had done? Was it something he told with remorse or as a joke? Ann had never said anything, not to her husband or a friend, not even in therapy or to her dad not long before he died when she caught herself humming "Hey There" only to feel his drugged gaze searching the room for someone not there. Not even after that day at Chuck E. Cheese when she realized it *was* Rosemary and she wanted to reach out and beg her forgiveness.

"Oh my," Rosemary had said, her face flushed bright pink when she saw Ann there with Sally. "Is that little Ann?"

She nodded and let go of Sally's hand so that she could dash to the big plastic hamster cage–looking structure she loved.

"What a darling child you have," she said, and Ann didn't correct her to say she was the substitute mother, just nodded a polite thanks and pointed to the young boy with pizza sauce all over his face.

"My grandbaby, Jonah." She laughed. "That's an old-sounding name for a baby, isn't it? But that's his name. I have four grandbabies." She held up four fingers, thin silver band held firm on her plump finger, and smiled at the older man sitting there easing the greasy milk straw into the child's mouth. "Oh, and this is Roland, my husband. Jonah is his daughter's boy." She turned to her husband. "I was friends with Ann's daddy when she was just a little skinny thing." She turned, her back to Roland and Jonah. "I was so sorry to hear about your dad," she whispered, and her large dark eyes filled with tears. "He was too young."

"Way too young." Ann nodded and looked away, up to where Sally was climbing and crawling behind the pink swirled plastic, lost in the maze of children. Ann knew her own marriage would likely not make it another calendar year, and in that moment the grief for all that was lost to her was somehow housed in the soft body of this woman whose real name she didn't even remember if she ever knew it at all.

"Well, he was very proud of you and Jimmy," she says. "I remember how he would walk way out in that lake with you on his back, whenever you asked to go."

She hadn't thought of that afternoon in years. They had gone back to Pongo Lake, only this time with fried chicken and biscuits and jam packed in a brown grocery bag from the Winn-Dixie. Ann clung to her dad's warm broad shoulders as he waded out into the lake. She remembered thinking his shoulders looked like luncheon meat, freckled and speckled that way, a ridiculous description but one she has thought of from time to time when shopping for cold cuts. "Deeper," she called, and when he was up almost to his neck, she scooted up with a foot on each shoulder and dove off and away from him.

"Poor man was scared to death," Rosemary said. "Couldn't swim a lick and standing all the way out there in the deep."

Ann didn't know he couldn't swim; she had not known until that moment.

"I was always worried I'd have to go in there or yell for a lifeguard, but he always came back." She laughed and shook her head. She wore a silver chain with an assortment of charms—a bird and a rolling pin, a boat, a moon, the ankh. "I hope he learned to swim. He swore to me he would."

"Did you know Dad couldn't swim?" Ann asks.

"No, but doesn't surprise me," Jimmy says and pats Kaycie's leg. "He didn't do much beyond work and golf and watch television."

"But those times he took us in the lake," Ann leans forward and waits for Jimmy to look at her.

"Ooh, we hate that lake," Kaycie says and laughs with the great confidence that plural pronoun gives her. "It's full of snakes and rednecks."

"Jimmy used to love it, though," Ann says. "In fact, the boy I knew loved the lake *and* scary movies."

"Well," Kaycie says, rearranging her magazines, "that boy is now a man. He may act a little silly when he gets with you but he is a grown man with a family to take care of and over fifty employees under him at the bank."

Ann resists the urge to make *family* plural, to say that Jimmy is living in another dimension—there with their beautiful young mother and a basket draped in linen with plump purple grapes on a china plate, but it is a place where nothing is real and no one is really happy and if they step too far into the lake they will all short-circuit, and if they walk to the flat edge of that happy family portrait, they will all fall off.

"MY BOY HAS a son, too," Rosemary said that day. "We got all boys and I love 'em to death but I'm still hoping for a little girl."

"Wild boys," the man, Roland, said. "And they love Martha too good to talk about." *Martha*. Had she ever even known? Martha.

"YOU KNOW," ANN says now, "that was an awful thing we did to Martha."

"Who's Martha?"

"Rosemary Looney."

"Dad never could have been happy with her," Jimmy shrugs. "She was nothing like Mom."

"But he *was* happy," she says.

Jimmy blinks and for the world looks just like their dad, and she tells him so, says she wants to go get some of the old photos to compare their features. She wants to show Kaycie what their baby might look like, show how Jimmy's ears were enormous before he grew into them, and how he used to suit up and pretend to be Bret Maverick.

"And I want to see the picture from the lake," Ann says. "I want to see if I'm remembering it right."

He tells her it's right where it's been for years, the far corner where they always kept the dog food and drink coolers, that he and Kaycie didn't want it hanging but of course hadn't felt like they could just throw it away. Ann opens the door and ventures down into the basement, the familiar damp smell, old lamps and chairs that used to be upstairs. "It'll just take a sec," she hears Jimmy tell Kaycie. She's upset because the dinner is going to be ruined if they don't eat soon and she's tired and hungry. Ann hears him offer a plea to her, the kind that seems to imply he's having to do this—humor and placate his little sister—the one afraid of the dark, the one inept in relationships like he used to be until he found and married her.

Ann goes to the far corner of the basement, and sure enough, there it is. Pongo Lake—the typical American family. Grapes and bread on a plate, her mother's dark hair curled close to her head, pearls at her throat. In the picture, Ann is studying her mother, hand reaching but not touching, and Jimmy is grinning, their dad's large hand on his shoulder. Ann remembers climbing on his back that day and holding close, begging him to go deeper, her cheek pressed against the speckled warmth of his skin. But that day he stopped at his waist and swung her off his back, urged her to swim on ahead, to show him what a fine swimmer she was.

With Martha on shore, he felt safer and had been able to go much farther. Martha had said his heart was beating like a jackhammer when he came up out of the water and collapsed on the blanket beside her. When she asked why on earth he did it, he said it was important that Ann not sense his fear, that she trust him to keep her safe.

"And I asked, 'who's keeping you safe?'" Martha laughed and instinctively reached and grabbed Ann's hand. "And he said, '*You* are.' That's what he said to me and he laughed great big and asked me to open him a beer." Martha shook her head and looked off toward the big plate windows and the busy parking lot where young families were coming and going. She took a deep breath and turned back.

"Your daddy said, 'And my Ann can swim like a little mud puppy.'" Martha squeezed Ann's hand and then patted her long-mended forearm. "A mud puppy, he called you, and he loved *my* hush puppies. Lord, he could put them away. He loved them." Her eyes filled with tears again and she blinked to straighten herself up when her husband called for her to look at Jonah dancing with Chuck E. Cheese. "He was a sweet man, your father." Ann nodded and wanted to fall into that body she had loved as a child, the same way she wishes she could fall into the portrait before her, just for a second, to fall into that time and kick the empty basket, to tell her mother to stop wasting time. *You can swim and won't,* Ann would say. *And you have less than three years to do it.*

She is staring into her dad's eyes, and with the focus on his face, the image of herself off to the side blurs and disappears from view as if she is no longer there, was never born, or maybe, as if with a great burst of freedom, she had run unafraid out into the lake all by herself. She wishes she had told her dad how sorry she was to have ruined his great chance at happiness, the chance for all of them to learn how it is supposed to feel, and she is speaking the words to him in her mind when she hears the door upstairs slam and click and then she prepares herself for what she knows is coming. The light goes out. She hears a shrill, giggling Kaycie telling Jimmy how bad he is, how foolish to reenact every childhood moment when they could be eating dinner and watching the movie that is from *her* childhood. "We never talk about *my* childhood," Kaycie says, and then there are the murmurs of their low conversation, apologies and promises. There is only blackness, and Ann takes long deep breaths while waiting for her eyes to adjust, the chairs and tables and books and furnace, the frame of the portrait, the long splintered steps up to the kitchen.

"I LOVED HIM very much," Martha said that day, and Ann wanted to say the obvious—*I know. He loved you, too*—but then she heard Sally's voice way up in the plastic pink-and-yellow cage, calling her name, screaming for help, and then the whole meeting and exchange was behind her, fuzzy like a dream, Martha saying she well understood that cry and pushing her in the direction of the crazy twisted tubes. Ann could hear Sally clearer now and the cries made her crawl faster, for a moment forgetting her own claustrophobia and grief and focusing only on the length of tube in front of her, the arms reaching out for safety. When she pulled Sally close to her, all crying stopped, and they began their descent with fussing, impatient children trying to push past them; Ann looked down and saw Martha staring up at the tubing, Jonah on her hip, but when they finally made it to the bottom and back into real light and air, she was gone.

"ANN?" JIMMY CALLS down in a singsong voice. "It's a joke. You know? Like old times." She resists the urge to keep him waiting and turns to the sound of his voice. There is something in the damp darkness and familiar smell that brings an odd sense of comfort and, with it, the knowledge that there is nothing more frightening than lost and crippled years. There is nothing scarier than *not* being willing to look into the unknown. She feels her way, small secure steps, until she sees her brother at the top of the stairs, young and boyish in the red skeletal glow of the flashlight he holds under his chin.

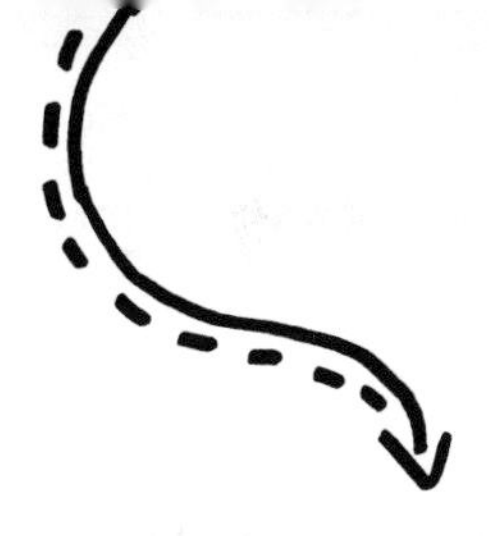

HAPPY ACCIDENTS

I HAVE ALWAYS been big on the end justifying the means, the karmic shuffle of it all—a path that allows for missteps and interesting discoveries, mistakes and second chances. A person who has made a lot of mistakes in life would be a fool to profess otherwise, and though I am a lot of things, a fool is not one. My desire to see a wrong turn become something wonderful is why I have long been a disciple of the television painter Bob Ross. I am a devoted follower. You may know him only as the man on PBS—*The Joy of Painting*—the pleasant-faced man with the Afro or Jewfro or Latinofro—whatever his origin might be—who speaks in such a kind and gentle voice about happy little clouds and little creatures hiding there in the nature he is painting. And yes, I know he is dead, but when I pop in a video it is like *poof*—resurrection. Bob said you could *use* your mistakes, like an accidental drop of black paint might become something beautiful or mysterious, the mouth of a cave or the shadow of a mountain.

I love Bob Ross and I also love the cheap substitute of paint by number. It's therapeutic and what I like to do when I don't want to think at all. As a result I have lots of shitty paintings all over my house—kittens with balls of yarn and puppies with gnawed-up shoes, horses with big butterflies alighting on their arched tails. These are cute enough, or would be if I was still eleven and waiting for good things to happen to me. Paint by number is an art form that jumps from the preadolescent to the elderly; it's an art form designed for BL (Before Life) and AL (After Life). I am just forty and should be In Life, right in the middle, and yet I remain a devoted follower.

I have gotten so fast with the process, ripping through those little plastic pots of oil paint, that I had to look for bigger and bigger paintings in hopes that they would hold me for awhile. Everyone who is into PBN knows that the biggest kits are always intricate whaling ships and *The Last Supper.* I did a whole harbor full of ships right after Stuart and I split up—I called it *The Fucked-Up Fleet from Hell.* I thought if I painted one more sail, I'd need to drink some arsenic and put myself out of my misery. So, I broke down and bought *The Last Supper.* Dark, dreary, and depressing. If somebody had offered me a little silver to sell them all out, I would've done it. And I certainly would have sold Stuart out in a flash, too, except for the fact that he sold me out first and not for what should have been my fair market value. I didn't even get the chance to say *Here's your hat but don't hurry* before he was clean across town and in a brand-new life with a brand-new girlfriend, this one without children, which didn't surprise me a bit. He wasn't good with his own child—why would he even care to try with someone else's?

"I mean it's not like we're married or anything," he had said. "It's not like I'm his father." He looked out the window to where Andrew was pushing the wheelbarrow, the handle about as tall as he was. "We both know we have hit the dead end." I watched those words coming out of his mouth and knew that he was right. I did know, had known, had a lifelong habit of picking dead ends because they were familiar to me, not good, just familiar, like the way an ex-prisoner starts to feel better—free and living on the outside—with the furniture pushed up against the wall and the floors hosed down and swept. It's not a pretty sight but it's dependable as clockwork. A life without any surprise is safe in its own way. You know if you stay within the lines and don't glom too much paint on your brush, your paint-by-number picture of a seagull squatting on a rugged post will turn out okay. Do you want to look at it for the rest of your life? Does it make you happy? Now those are different questions altogether.

I keep thinking that if I do enough paint by numbers and keep watching my tapes of Bob that my artistic ability will take shape. One day I will wake up and instinctively know how to create light on the water, wind in the mane, deep furling creases in the robe of Judas. So far this miracle has not occurred. And I guess things like artistic talent cannot be easily explained. You can't explain talent just like you can't teach the ability to love. People are forever asking about my quilt designs, which by the way, actually earn me good money when I settle in and do them. I am known for my crazy quilts and the good eye I have for piecing together colors and textures that people would never think of combining. In one of my prize-winning quilts, I cut up Stuart's tuxedo he'd left hanging in my closet and coupled it with scraps of antique barkcloth from the drapes that had hung in my grandmother's bedroom for seventy-five years. I named it *The Night Has a Thousand Eyes.* I cut the satin lapels from the tux into circles, like pupils—some dilated, others not—and sprinkled them onto other fabrics—bits of an old butter-colored chenille spread my parents owned, worn soft flannel from my own Lanz nightgown. The centers of the pale pink peonies—some white, some yellow, from my grandmother's drapes—also resembled eyes, dappled and searching. I never explain the name I give to anything. I never told how every bit of fabric laid out there had been witness to the life of a bed. These fabrics knew the routines, the cries and murmurs, of three generations. These fabrics held secrets that I myself would never know, ones I didn't want to know. I was both drawn to and repulsed by the thought. I didn't want to imagine my grandparents' naked bodies entwined in the darkness those rich-colored peonies had shed, and I didn't want to picture my parents beneath the soft warmth of that chenille, a fabric that completely betrayed the real texture of what was a sad and hopeless relationship, two people light-years apart but choosing to share the same space. I was the glue that held them together. I was the mistake that shaped the rest of their lives: her sad attempts, his bitter regret.

Divorce would have been such a gift for my parents. I wanted that for them. When I was eight, the music teacher at my school got one and it seemed to make her really happy. People whispered about her but she didn't act like she cared; she just kept singing and looking beautiful, like a plump, black-haired Julie Andrews. I remember sitting on Santa's lap late one December afternoon in front of Taylor's Hardware on Main Street. He said, "What do you want, little girl?" My first thought was to move next door with the beautiful Palandjian sisters; I wanted their exotic name and sweet fun-loving mother for my own. There was a boy dressed like a gunslinger pointing his six-shooter at me like I better hurry up so I leaned back against Santa's warm padded chest and tilted my mouth near his ear. My parents were standing right there in front of a stack of snow shovels that nobody in this neck of the woods would ever need, looking tired and bored—she was probably wishing she was over at JCPenney trying on clothes that would make her look like a teenager and he was wishing he was out drinking something and working on that old Thunderbird he swore would someday be a prize but never was. "A divorce," I whispered in his warm creased ear and then lay my head down while the cowboy made sounds like he just shot a whole round into my heart.

"What?" Santa sounded surprised and tried to look me in the eye but I held onto him another minute. He smelled good and I liked his fat body. "What did you say, honey?"

"Thumbelina," I said then. "The little one, and also Incredible Edibles."

STUART WAS WEARING his tuxedo when I first met and fell for him. How can you not notice a handsome man in a tuxedo sitting in a little elementary school chair, his long legs stretched way out into the room. It was back-to-school night. I am the school nurse and I had just given a presentation about what constituted the need for a parent to come and take somebody home: fever over one hundred degrees, severe sprains and broken bones, vomiting more than once. I explained how sometimes a child might throw up out of pure excitement or one too many times around on the whirligig or as part of a chain reaction set off by another child's vomiting in the cafeteria. However, I stressed, beyond such spontaneous and event-prompted nausea, it is very important for a sick child to be sent home. Not only is a vomiting child contagious but he also feels humiliated stretched out and moaning on a cot for others to see.

I tried to remind the crowd of parents seated in the cafeteria what it felt like to be a child. I believe that whole thing about those who don't remember history are forced to repeat it. I have a poster like that in my office right beside one of a frightened kitten hanging from the limb of a tree with the caption HANG IN THERE. I think if a parent can remember what it felt like to be frightened and alone then maybe they can protect their kids a little bit better, keep them from having to go through all the bad shit they did.

"Life is scary enough," I told them, "without being sick on top of it." I looked up and saw Stuart was now leaning into the open doorway, tie undone, overcoat open. He was right beside a traffic poster that said, LOOK BOTH WAYS BEFORE CROSSING. WHEN IN DOUBT, DON'T, and I should have remembered that a half hour later when he came up to me, juice and cookies in hand, to suggest we go get a real drink somewhere before he headed out to his black-tie event. His little girl—a second grader who had never been sick at school and thus was unknown to me—lived with her mother full-time. He only showed up at these things to "fuck with the ex a little," let her know he wasn't entirely out of the picture. It was a negative hidden picture, like if Bob Ross had painted a rattlesnake down in the bushes beside the front door of your painted house instead of a tiny nest of sparrows. I should have taken heed. I knew better even as I accepted his invitation and all the ones that followed.

"Why don't you realize that I, like most humans inhabiting this planet, am not inferior to you," I once asked when he was explaining at great length how I *should* have done everything I'd done that day from wash the clothes to cook the meal to wear my hair. We had been together for about a year and this was a pattern. Stuart is one of those people you marvel at—not because he's so great but because he thinks he's so great. People who meet him for just little encounters are fooled for a long time. Those who actually get to the end of the prerecorded infomercial—who he knows, where he's been, why he's admired by so many—realize that there's nothing else there. That's it. Th-th-th-that's all folks. What you see is what you get. No surprises hiding there after all. If Stuart was a paint by number, he'd be *The Last Supper:* dark, depressing, swigging wine, eating way too many carbs, and, of course, betraying. Constantly betraying. Not me so much as himself. Stuart wants to be loved and wanted by everyone and he wants to accomplish this by doing nothing. Whenever I mentioned his daughter and how nice it would be for him to plan something for her, a trip to the zoo, dinner out, how I would go, too, if that made it easier, he would say *good idea* or *yeah, sure* or any number of those quick replies people give when they want you to shut up and leave them alone.

By then, of course, I noticed her all the time—Charlotte—a thin little girl with dark curly hair and big brown eyes. Every day at recess she sat in the same swing, the same little red-haired boy beside her, and every day her mother, far more attractive than Stuart had painted her, was waiting on the sidewalk to walk her home. Stuart had told me that he and his ex often went weeks without speaking, that it was like living in a tomb and sleeping with a corpse. And all I could think was how much better then that this child is no longer breathing their stale bitter air. How wonderful it must be for her to wake and find her mother alone in the bed.

Children who grow up in such a household learn early how to clown and try to make everyone happy or they learn to apologize for things they didn't do in hopes of ending the tension so a kind of normal life can return. And some parents let them do this—soak up blame and responsibility like a sponge when what they really need is for someone to pick them up and wring out all the toxins they've absorbed. It isn't theirs to carry. They are the emotional placentas, struggling to protect their own vital parts while sucking up and storing others' neglectful nasty habits.

When I saw Andrew for the first time, his warm wet body placed atop my stomach, cord still connecting us, I promised him that I would do my best. That I hoped to always admit my mistakes and try to make up for them. That I never wanted to dump my problems on him. That I wanted to try and explain things in a way that made sense, try and explain what's beneath the surface of it all. Now, I show him how before I do a paint by number, I usually paint a message onto the canvas first, just in case anyone ever bothers to look or more so just so I know it is there, like a worry stone or lucky penny in your pocket, a wish that repeats itself in your head. Or I take out my plastic brain mold, which I have used to entertain him and kids at school every Halloween and other holidays, too. It's a Jell-O mold and if you buy Berry Blue or Grape and add just the slightest bit of cream, it comes out a perfect brainy gray. I put messages within the brain, little notes wrapped in Saran Wrap that he discovers like fortune cookies: MY MOTHER LOVES ME TO PIECES, or, I AM GOING TO BE A GREAT POET, or, BEWARE! IGOR GRABBED THE WRONG BRAIN!

YOU MIGHT LOOK at me now and wonder why I didn't get sucked on down Misery Canal. Why did I not become my sad shell of a mother taking pills for ailments that likely didn't exist and hiding behind racks of clothes to try on and hoard while tired sales ladies on commission told her she was beautiful? Why didn't I pack a bag and flee as Stuart had from his marriage and then from me, as my father might as well have done all those years ago when he sat in a dark garage in a car that would never move again? Flight. Escape. It's such a simple and common story. Why am I not sitting off somewhere saying *I'll be quiet* or zonked out of my gourd or living a total lie? Well, for one thing I have a good job surrounded by children who need me, and I have projects it will take me years to finish as I practice the teachings of Bob Ross, and I have Andrew. Above all else, I have Andrew.

It was when I was pregnant that I discovered Bob. I was told that his voice would soothe and ease me into sleep better than trying to read the Bible, which was another recommendation for insomnia that I had received. Bob was better than NyQuil or Benadryl, neither of which was even an option while pregnant. Bob lulled me to sleep each afternoon, me with eyes barely held open searching the pines off at the edge of the mountain for the little nest of birds he assured me was there while Andrew paddled his little limbs within, his tight round rump twisting and pushing against my ribs. "Happy creatures," Bob said. "There to find if you look real hard." I wanted to live in Bob's world. I didn't even crave that much—light, air, occasional laughter. I would lie there like beached blubber murmuring, "goddamnit Bobby, I want happy clouds. I want to be a happy creature." What he could do every day with a blank canvas amazed me. It was like painting all of one little number of paint at one time in a PBN without having the box to show you exactly what you were doing. What's more, Bob's technique of applying one color right on top of another was called "wet on wet," which I found so erotically charged even there in my condition. Wet on wet sounded to me like slick skin-slapping sex, the quality of which I had not experienced nearly enough in my life. I love how Bob never abandoned what began with wet on wet even when it was looking messy. In Bob's world there were no mistakes, only "happy accidents." Take that smear of yellow where the reflection of your sun looks stupid and unnatural and turn it into a giant sunflower. Take your deformed-looking dog and just smear it all out into a little tranquil pond. Bob could dive into a pile of shit and come out riding a silver pony.

ANDREW IS EIGHT now and expressed very little emotion when Stuart packed up and left. "It's not like he's my real dad," he said, and he looked at me as if I might give him more information about his real father, the fiction I have created to fill the void of what is not entirely known—a kind but otherwise really boring mechanic who taught me what parts to point to under the hood so I wouldn't be taken advantage of, the medical student doing a month's rotation in ophthalmology when I was finishing up nursing school, the married landscape designer who spent half a summer wandering the grounds of my apartment complex, taking in and examining the various women who lived there the same way he did the grade and slope of the terrain. He was famous for complimenting women on their buds and bushes. And of course we all thought he was totally full of shit but too completely good-looking for his own good, or our good I guess. For all I know he's still hoeing rows and planting seeds, like an old mule who only knows one path of dirt.

But Andrew's father—by my account—was a brilliant young man who after being in the Peace Corps for two years became a war correspondent during the Gulf War. No sooner did we marry and have a beautifully memorable honeymoon in the Galapagos Islands (I saw a television special on this and knew all I needed to know) than he was reported missing and presumed dead. The only question Andrew asked was why we didn't use his father's last name, Perdue—we were in the grocery store when he asked—and I said it was just too painful a reminder of the life I almost had but then didn't. I told how his father was an only child whose parents had both died when he was young so we were all that was left of his family. When Andrew wanted to know where his dad was buried, I pulled out a photo of my childhood home and pointed where the sun was about to drop behind the thick pine woods between my house and the high school. "I sprinkled him here," I said. "It's where he proposed to me." I told him how you can't see it in the photo but if you walk there in the woods there is an old rusted-out buggy where as children his dad and I sat and pretended we were heading west to find gold and eternal happiness. I told him how wonderful it was to be hidden there in the trees.

I'd be lying if I said I wasn't a little angry when Stuart left, even though it was inevitable and I was glad it happened. It was more about feeling responsible for what had failed. I had spent my life feeling that way and *that* is what really made me angry. I was sick and tired of making other people's mistakes look good when no one was helping out with mine. "How did this happen?" my mother asked when she saw me pregnant with Andrew. "What on earth am I going to say to people?" She spoke with great authority and arrogance as if she might be the mother equivalent to the *Mona Lisa.*

Painting is a very good way to handle things like anger. Sometimes, I paint like a maniac while I go over things in my head. Sometimes my head is XXX rated. I do things in my head that would get me the death penalty in this state. And that's harmless, right? Paint a little on Jesus's beard while imagining all that will never happen but *could.* All the ways I might force people to see and hear me as I really am, all my parts and all my layers.

I am someone who needs to be aware of what is under the surface. My grandmother's old quilts, I found, often conceal a quiltface under the one showing. I am intrigued when a painting is discovered under another. And I love those little Russian nesting dolls—something inside of something inside of something. A secret message tucked back, layered for a later revelation. It's history—the organs beneath the skin—the heart. It's the belief that there is something out there that will save me.

"Nothing lasts forever," Stuart said when he left. It scares me to think so, but I think there was a time I would have begged him to stay, changed myself into something I wasn't to avoid conflict and change. I likely would have taken the blame—a problem I have wrestled with my whole life, so conditioned to assume that I didn't deserve anything better, that once I messed up I was out of the game, like misspelling a word in a spelling bee or severing a main artery out in the middle of nowhere. I was asked by a shrink once what my worst fear was, and I didn't even have to think to answer. "My worst fear," I told him, "is that I will stumble upon a crime and confess that I am responsible." I am someone desperate for resolutions, a sense of completion and well-being. I want to tell people how everything is going to be okay, to reassure them that there is light up ahead even when they can only see the darkness. The glass is half full. When you find yourself neck deep in shit, there is bound to be a pony nearby.

"That's fairy tale bullshit," Stuart told me on more than one occasion, when I expressed the hope of what was waiting for me out there in the future.

"There's no brass ring," my father often said. "One bad turn just leads to another. You automatically sink lower than you might have been with no hope of getting back." He looked at my mother as he said this.

If there is a hell and I am forced to go there, then I will be surrounded by negative and pessimistic people. I will hear them complain and whine, judge and sentence everyone and everything around them. And in between their tirades I will be presented with books missing their final chapters, movies that blip out just before the final scene, elaborate recipes that don't tell what temperature the oven should be. No situation will have a resolution; there will be no glimmer of a future.

BUT FOR NOW, I love nothing better than sitting on the little cot in my office, my fingers smoothing tangled hair and tear-stained dirty faces. I tell them that they will feel better very soon. The fever will break and the bone will heal. Their parents would never forget to pick them up. "There's traffic, so much traffic," I say. "There is nothing on the whole planet they love any better than you."

Some might say that my life has been one long series of mistakes and accidents, but Bob Ross has taught me otherwise. I can take myself and turn me into something really good. He has taught me that it's important to know what's possible. He was only fifty-two when he died, though his show continued to play day after day long after. Some might have seen these repeats as a sad thing, the long good-bye. But I saw and continue to see them as a wonderful resurrection. Day after day, he springs back to life with the promise of something new. He's a lot like Jesus when you think about it—the second chance, the promise of something better, the beard.

Now when I paint, I leave little spaces in the trees for Bob. I like to think he's back up in the woods there painting up a frenzy. Or he's cooking a nice gourmet meal for the two of us to sit and enjoy at the end of a long day. We are just friends, of course, bound by our artistic sensibilities. He has a wife he loves and I really am not attracted to him in that wet-on-wet kind of way, though I am not above thinking he might have a friend he wants me to meet. He's there thinking of all the nice things he will say when he sees me: How he sees beneath my skin and bones to my very soul. How I deserve so much more than I have seen thus far. He says the trick is to go just one little brushstroke at a time, that what I am making of Andrew—that little wet-on-wet happy accident—is a great work in progress and worth every minute I spend there. He tells me to look before crossing, to hang in there. He says every day is a good day to be alive.

VIEW-MASTER

THE EX-WIFE'S PICTURE hangs among others near the radiator in Roger's office. Theresa has trouble *not* looking at the photo even though she has studied and memorized every detail with a kind of tormenting curiosity. The other photos are linked to Roger's commercial real estate business—photo after photo of Roger shaking hands with local celebrities, the mayor, the anchor for the local news, and Tripp Trout, owner of a seafood franchise who has never been seen without his fish mask. There are probably twenty such photos.

Beside the ex-wife is a younger, leaner Roger with dark hair and no lines around his eyes. He's smiling, and there is not a trace of worry or discontent; his hand cups the bare shoulder of the woman beside him: his wife, his mate. Her blond hair is shoulder length and feathered back from her face; her jeans are worn and flared, her feet bare, and she rests one leg over his. She leans in so their heads are touching. His other hand, wedding ring visible, is on her thigh as he hugs her close. He's wearing an old flannel shirt he still owns, one Theresa used to toss on in the middle of the night or after showering. She has not worn it since recognizing its connection to the past.

His daughter, just a toddler then, is in a little pink jacket off to the side. Her hair is yanked into high pigtails, something Theresa has heard Roger laugh and tease her about when they talk on the phone—"Those tight pigtails did something to your brain, honey," he always says. Now the daughter is in college on the West Coast. Theresa has not met her, though they have chatted on the phone in a friendly but awkward fashion until he is able to pick up—about Roger's work or the weather or Elsa, the old golden retriever who was just a puppy at the time of the divorce. The ex-wife, though several relationships and houses and careers beyond the marriage, continues to call and check in.

In the photo, they are a family of three on vacation in the mountains; dark shapes looming behind them in late-afternoon light. There is a history behind them and several years still ahead. Theresa looks once more at their entwined limbs, their child, the place Roger has said *they* should visit sometime. It was where he had spent his childhood vacations. It was *his* place first. Theresa holds eye contact with the ex-wife and thinks: I *am here and you are way back there.*

But Roger is in both places.

"OH, YOU WOULDN'T have liked me then," Roger said when he caught her studying the photo. She wanted to ask him why he kept it hanging, but before she could figure out how to ask, he was already telling the story of the day, his daughter covered in poison ivy by the end of it, the oatmeal bath and calamine lotion he bought and brought back to the motel room, where his wife was studying for either the LSAT or to go to graduate school in library science—he couldn't remember which. She never pursued either one. What he could remember is that she didn't want him to watch the ballgame on television or touch or talk to her. He described a perfectly awful time, and yet the photo remained like a door left wide open. Theresa wanted to ask, *Would you go back and fix it all if you could?*

Before Roger, most of her relationships were built on convenience, the result of sporadic and fleeting moments of boredom or lust. She had resisted an early conventional union that might—with good health and luck—lead to a golden wedding anniversary, and she had resisted repeating her own unhappy childhood by not having any children of her own. Instead she had thrown all her time and energy into her work, assuring herself that someday she would find what was right for her, comforted by the idea of comfort.

"No one has everything," she was reminded countless times by friends who were getting married and having children. They were trying to emphasize her successful landscaping business, which is how she met Roger. She went from selling small window box and herb garden designs at the Farmers' Market to landscaping bank buildings and city plazas. Her brief engagement and a couple of meaningless relationships were all mixed up in her mind with abelia and dwarf gardenias and the Bradford pear trees all over town whose varying sizes documented her career.

When she sees Roger in the photograph, she feels oddly homesick. It's the same feeling she had as a kid staring into her View-Master at images of places so real she wanted to claim them as her own. As a ten-year-old, her favorite reel was the one of Yellowstone Park—hot springs and sunsets, red rock ledges so steep and close she was afraid to take a step while viewing. In the one of Old Faithful there was a man in plaid Bermuda shorts and a white dress shirt with his whole family in tow, which dated the photo and invaded her space. They did not belong in her life. She loved the moose in the snow, the almost navy sky, but most of all she loved the black bears, so real she wanted to reach out and stroke their fur.

• • •

THERE IS ANOTHER photo of a much younger Roger in front of the old E&R Drive-In before it was torn down and replaced by a Food Lion. It was a fixture in the area, catering to the Saturday night dates of a three-county region. Roger was one of the many supporters trying to save it. And so was she. Somewhere in the huge gathering of people spilling beyond the frame, she knows she is there. So is Tripp Trout, Roger has said, but very few people know what he looked like before the mask.

"So we could have met twenty years ago," he said. "Been together so long we'd be sick of each other or maybe in counseling by now."

"You were already married."

"And you were engaged."

"You said I wouldn't have liked you back then."

"But I lied. What were you wearing?"

"Levi's, T-shirt, Birkenstocks," she said. "I was real original."

"Wait. I *do* remember you," he said. "I tried to pick you up but you ignored me."

"No, I tried to pick *you* up but you said you had to ask your wife."

NOW THEY REFER often to *the day we never met* and have pinpointed other possible intersections, the ghosts of their younger selves acting out all the parts they never got to play. In fact she once drove by that place in the mountains where he used to go. She might have stopped for gas and walked into the very store he went in to buy that oatmeal bath. She could have met him then. She could have said, *Bad day, huh?*

How much time do you have and I'll tell you.

I have more time than I know what to do with.

SHE TURNS OFF the light in his office and makes her way to the darkened bedroom where Roger is stretched out sleeping, Elsa snoring at his feet. She reaches out to familiar shapes, window, wall, brittle unnourished ficus she is attempting to resurrect, chair with his jeans slung over the back, table where his reading glasses are folded. She finds the footboard, Elsa's blanket. Fur, flannel, skin; knee, thigh, hip. His chest moves up and down under the weight of her hand.

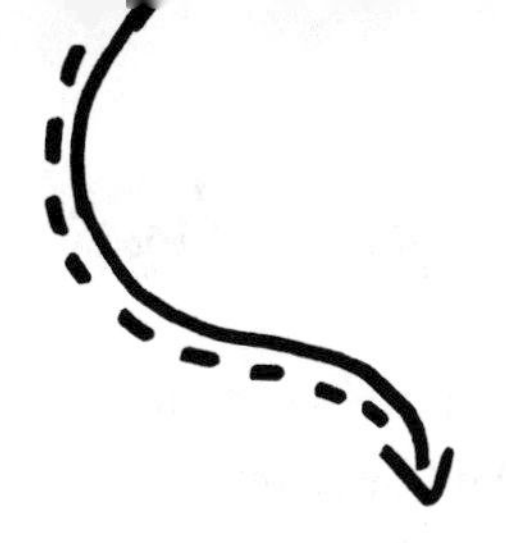

PS

Dear Dr. Love,

By now you have gotten several letters from me and this will probably be the last. I don't care that you never respond. In fact, I'm glad that you don't, because if you did, it would show a weakness in your professional ethics. In all my other letters, I have been trying to explain myself a little better because I always felt like maybe you liked Jerry more than you liked me. And what is it about human nature that makes us all want to be the one liked the most? In those other letters I was still trying to convince you how I was the right one, but the truth is that now so much time has passed that I just don't give a shit. The right/wrong stalemate is what keeps people in your office for way too long. I thought I might wrap it all up in my mind by writing you this *final* letter. And I will tell the truth—not that I haven't told the truth in the past, I have, but let's just say I also lied.

What has been consistent and honest in all my letters is how I don't think your name works and I still think you should change it. You might say it led you to do what you do, and you might mention other people with prophetic names like Judge Learned Hand or someone I knew named Clay Potts, who still makes mugs and stuff to sell by the highway, but I never liked the way your name feels like a bad joke to all those people who are struggling with their marriages. Maybe you should change it to Dr. Apathy, which they (the 1960s shrink set) said was the opposite of love instead of hate, and I absolutely agree with this. In fact, I think if they ever remake *The Night of the Hunter,* which is one of my very favorite movies (or was until Jerry got religious), they might rethink the tattoos that the preacher has on his hands. Lord, Robert Mitchum was scary there using his hands to show the fight between love and hate, and him a cold-blooded killer hiding behind Scripture. But imagine a preacher (or a marriage counselor) with hands saying LOVE and APATHY. You love all those little games; you can put your hands behind your back and say, *Pick.*

Anyway, when you last saw me, I did not look good. In fact, I looked like shit on a stick. Most of us coming in and out of your home office did, you know. I know you think that you have it all figured out so people don't see one another—five-minute intervals and in one door and out another—it *is* a big-ass house—but truth is, I rarely made an immediate exit. I would stop off in your little bathroom there at the front to splash water on my face and get myself looking good enough to go pick the kids up from school. Sometimes, you may recall, I would even have to excuse myself during a session. You might have thought I was being avoidant but truth is I was bored. I suspect being bored and having your mind wander during marriage counseling is not a good sign. I would suspect that that level of boredom should say something big. You should tell people right up front how if they're bored then probably the best thing for everybody is to call it quits. Don't take their money, don't make them sit there and say stupid things back and forth.

Anyway, I did like sitting there in your bathroom, the way the white noise enveloped me and kept me from hearing all that Jerry was probably saying about me while I wasn't there. He probably said things like how I often rearranged the furniture or changed the lightbulbs to get a better feel to the room, or how I didn't check the cabinets and pantry before going shopping and how he was tired of me buying things like sugar or mayonnaise or a big can of pepper for fear there was none back at home. He didn't like that I bought Chef Boyardee either even though the kids love it. Who doesn't? I don't like being told what is *right* and what is *wrong*.

"Do you know how many bags of sugar are in that pantry?" he would often ask, and I would say, "No! how many?" like it was a game, which made him mad enough to pull out a bunch of bags and stack them there on the floor like we might be getting ready for a flood. Then I might say something like *Do you know how many* Sports Illustrateds *are in the bathroom getting all wet and soggy?* or *Do you know how you bruised my arm when you grabbed me so hard during sex the last time we had it?* But you know better because you know Jerry. Those would be my fantasy marriage-counseling complaints, where I might also have big stinky jock sneakers in the hall and a man thinking of all the new ways he might go about satisfying me.

In reality I would say, *Do you know how many daily devotional books and Mensa quizzes are neatly stacked on the shelf in the bathroom? Do you know where the antibacterial cleanser might be or that thing you use to scrub your tongue?* Jerri did not like for his tongue to look like a normal tongue. I don't even know who thought of a tongue brush but I am open-minded enough that I said if he needed to do that it was okay with me, that I personally didn't feel the need to scrape my own but certainly I wouldn't judge him for doing so.

You (and the whole planet Earth) were always talking about Venus and Mars, and I got it. It was like the tongue brush or the way I like toilet paper backed up to the wall and Jerry likes it spinning off the front. Different strokes and so on. But that explanation just didn't work when it came to religion, mainly because Jerry kept trying to *save* me. "From what, Jerry?" I must have said forty times. "What are you saving me from?"

I guess coming to you was like going somewhere like Saturn or Uranus to work it out. Remember when I observed that? And then I said how sometimes a planet is *not* a planet, like Pluto for instance. All these years we thought it was a planet only to find out it wasn't. Clearly I was too subtle for both of you because you didn't do more with my observation and Jerry just shook his head and winked at you as if to say, *You see? You see how off she is?* and I said, "Up Uranus." Do you remember that? I'm hoping that you can picture us there that day: Jerry and Hannah from three suburbs over.

Anyway, I think that marriage vows should include an escape clause that says the contract is broken if one party up and makes a big switch in religion or politics or aesthetic taste. I mean, it just isn't fair, and there needs to be an easier way out. There's all that discussion about marriage versus civil union. Well, I think everybody needs to be civil and I think anybody that wants to call a relationship a marriage should have the right to do so. I'm an open-minded person and these days a more honest person, so I'll just go ahead and tell you that you were not our first counselor. In the beginning, we—like so many who come to you—were just hoping for an honest appraisal, like when you take your car in. Do they open the hood and just close it with disgust, like the way people often describe cancer: *They opened and then just closed her right up?* Or do they say, *Well, this vehicle might not have been the* best *choice for you, but there's miles left in her. Keep her in tires and oil and she'll probably get you where you need to go?* Or do they say, *Ah yes, she's a beauty and if you just pay attention to the subtle sounds of this complex engine then she'll be purring for life and won't you feel proud to have a hand on her wheel?*

My first choice of a therapist was Ashley Hoffman, but he is so brilliant and popular, a patient has to die for you to get an appointment. So I chose a Dr. Levine for his good Jewish name because I had decided that the only way I could get some objectivity to counterbalance what had become Jerry's religious fervor was to find a good atheist or agnostic or Unitarian. Well, that is not information that you can find anywhere in an advertisement. So, I thought I could go the more subtle route and look for a good Jewish name, which I did, only to have another bad joke played on me. Dr. Levine's mother, it turned out, was a Baptist, and that's how he had grown up down in Alabama, with Mr. Levine nowhere in sight. His accent was thicker than mine and he used the words *bless* and *blessing* all the goddamn time. Jerry liked him, of course. Jerry likes talking to men better than he likes dealing with women even though he won't admit it. I know you picked up on this, too, but I'll come back to that. I felt that this lack of separation of church and marital state was a big conflict of interest. I wanted to tell Dr. Levine that I wanted to sue his ass for false advertisement because there is a great and rich Hebrew heritage in the field of psychotherapy but, of course, I didn't. Instead of that I told Jerry that Dr. Levine had to let all his clients go because he was suffering a nervous breakdown of sorts and then I opened the Yellow Pages, closed my eyes, and found you. The name *Love* sounded prophetic at the time. Ha ha.

But I did like how you always had the daily paper and *People* magazine in your bathroom, except sometimes when I started reading, I forgot that I had to go back in there and hear what a difficult person I am. Remember that time you had to come and get me and I told you I was feeling sick? Really I was reading about David Koresh and thinking how Jerry's new religion was getting on my nerves but at least he wasn't *that* bad. Not yet anyway. Of course, I wanted to know what to be looking for in case the turn he'd already taken got worse.

Love or apathy. The game of marriage. The game of monogamy. Some would say *monotony*. You take turns. You go round and round. Sometimes you have to pay a penalty or lose your turn. Still, it's not easy to make a big change and that is what I was often thinking while collecting myself and watching others coming and going. The people I saw leaving who looked good and all together were already done deals I suspect. You could tell the ones who already knew they were out of there and were just going through the motions to appease the other one enough to get a better deal during the divorce—more money, more time with the kids. I mean, so many people go to counseling for the kids, and that's a good thing when it works—kind of like a sermon when it's good and inspirational and you can use what you hear—but it can also become selfish. All that money that could go to college and all that time that could go to taking them fun places. I mean, I spent a hell of a lot to get bored and wander around getting creeped out by your spooky violent and primitive art stuff.

I wish I could get all that money back from you. One day I added it up and it totaled at least a new car, which I really need these days. Do you remember how Jerry wanted to have me diagnosed crazy? And then how he was hoping I had brain cancer? "Something is causing your abstract thoughts," he said. I mean no offense, well, actually I do mean a little offense, I never understood why you didn't get pissed off and tell him to let you tend to your own business. I mean, you listened to him sitting there in all his born-again glory. He would have loved a reason to have me drugged or lobotomized so I'd just drool and go along with whatever he said whenever he said it.

And I am someone who does believe in the higher power of necessary medication. Amen. Like there are times when a smidgen of this or that is just what you need. I loved the feel of Demerol when I was in labor and don't know what I would have done without that epidural, scream out lots of terrible things, I suspect, which I did anyway. And this drug they give you with a colonoscopy is just a dream—you're relaxed on one side, wide awake and watching television. I wanted to nominate myself for an Emmy. And I believe in spiritual highs, too. What I don't believe in is someone having the power to dictate someone else's spirituality or aesthetic code. Like if I hate corduroy, that is *my* business, not his.

But I did not *marry* a born-again person and so, yes, I did have a problem when he up and got all religious on me. It was just another way to control and manipulate. You aren't smart enough because you aren't Mensa material. You aren't neat and clean enough even when you say you're trying. You aren't saved because you haven't cried and humiliated yourself by confessing to the congregation all the awful things you have done in life so they can heal, bless, and forgive you. That is *not* who I married. I mean, I didn't marry a luxury vehicle, I know that, but I did marry what I thought was your basic white stripped-down Corolla. I married Jerry Barnes, Toyota dealer, who in grade school was told that he scored in the genius range on some stupid aptitude test and has spent his whole life doing things like Rubik's Cube to prove it. He was a lot of hot air but nice enough and kind of cute on a good day—a lot shorter than me but I didn't think much of it especially since Dudley Moore and Susan Anton were an item around the time we were dating. People would say, "There's Dudley and Susan," and I liked that. I know that's stupid but I was also only about twenty-two years old and still going to school for interior design. I liked a margarita on a Saturday afternoon and a glass of wine while cooking dinner, and so did Jerry, but now he is a teetotaler. He can't do anything halfway or in moderation. Forgive my diversion but thinking about first meeting Jerry made me think of my neighbor's little Chihuahua, who is all the time trying to mount my Lab, Sheba, and I say, "There's Dudley and Susan." But now Dudley is dead and very few people even remember that he was ever with Susan Anton. I loved that movie *Arthur* myself. Jerry did, too, back when he was Jerry.

But it wasn't enough for Jerry to be normal Jerry, he had to always be into this or that. There was always a new hobby and he'd go at it full tilt for a few months and then would move on to another interest. He was into Sudoku and then pottery, model trains, and beer making. He wanted to take dancing lessons and then he got interested in a kind of tag wrestling that involved grown men moving all around one another and then grabbing and holding. I referred to it as "homoerotic dance," and he accused *me* of not being open-minded, and I just said, "Whatever." I told him that I'd never in my life had any trouble finding somebody who wanted to dance with me and he should remember that.

I am realistic enough to know that there are often psychological or subconscious reasons people go where they go and make the choices they make. I mean, even though he tells people I'm not *saved*, I did grow up going to church, right? And where I went there was a virtual feast of questionable things happening, so I'd be a total fool *not* to question. Youth directors and choir directors and assistant this and that who took a "special interest" in the children. Some liked young girls and some liked young boys. "(I'm a) Boy Watcher." Remember that song? Or worse, remember those sunglasses? A slit of polarized glass so that no one could tell where you were looking—creepy. And that's why I told Jerry that if he was having some thoughts in those directions that he needed to spend some time with himself and his thoughts and his impulses and come to a personal decision. And of course, that is when he came to the personal decision that he needed to rededicate his life to the Lord and that he needed to bring me along with him. I might add that this is a place where people want to heal the homosexuals and those who are prochoice.

You must get tired of hearing the same old thing over and over because of course it isn't really about the toothpaste cap left off or the toilet seat up or who loaded the dishwasher last. All that little nitpicky stuff usually means is: *You get on my fucking nerves so bad I can't stand it.* It means: *What happened to the person I thought I was marrying?* It means: *You don't like the cat so I don't like you.* It means: *I pretend I'm asleep when your hand brushes my back. I pretend your hand belongs to somebody else.*

Now, I'm not trying to tell you your business, but I think if I were you, I would just have a series of questions that lead to a big yes or no answer. Should I get divorced? Ding ding ding—the answer is yes. I mean, I realize that a lot of people go into your business for a little self-help, and that's where you might very well overlap a little bit with Jerry being born again. People with mental and emotional problems very often seek refuge in the church and the field of psychology. I'd say about 80 percent of you probably do that. And that's fine for a personal weakness to lead you to a calling. I can dig it. I mean, that is what led me to interior design after all. Everyone in my town would tell you that I grew up in a rat hole firetrap and that my chosen profession was all about bringing color and clarity and order into a life of chaos. I mean, my mother couldn't help that she was one of those people who never cleaned house and never cared if anything matched or not. And my dad was a fireman, who should've known not to have stacks of paper everywhere with both of them chain-smoking, but the cobbler's children go barefoot, like your girl I met one day on a bathroom trip, but I'll get back to that in a minute.

By the way, if you are actually reading this letter, don't think you can charge me for the time like that lawyer keeps doing every time I e-mail or call him back to answer a question he asked me. Just the other day he said, "How are you doing?" And I said I wasn't saying unless he stopped the clock and kept it stopped until I was done. I think it was hard for him in that moment to figure out what part was human and what part was not. It was the only time I had ever heard him pause in conversation, like he'd shorted out or something.

Some of my conversations with my lawyer have reminded me of those little games you had us play, which you need to know right up front do not work at all. I think you'd have to be a total idiot or someone who takes Mensa quizzes regularly to fall for such simplistic crap. I mean, anybody who ever saw *Annie Hall* knows to read the subtext.

You look so pretty today. (Like a bitch who spent too much at Nordstrom.)

Why thank you, love. (Fuck you.)

What I know now is that, just by way of thinking those thoughts, I should not have continued shelling out two hundred bucks a pop to you. I'd have done just as well to rent a boxing ring for an hour. There's a test right there. Get in the ring and if you are—in a great moment of anger—willing to drive your fist into the face of someone you promised to cherish forever (especially if the genetics have worked such that those are now the same eyes you associate with your children), well then, Houston, we've got a problem.

So I WONDER about you. Like at the end of the day, do you put your feet up and tell your wife all about us? Do you open a bottle of wine and snuggle on that big divan up in your room (I made a wrong turn once going to the bathroom and will get back to that) and say thank God I am not living such an unhappy existence? Does it make you love her more? She looks a bit older than you and so I did wonder (when I saw the photo on your dresser) if she had had a husband before you and how you had adjusted to that or if you all have some different kind of marriage like mentor/mentee or mother and child. Truth is, you seemed a little too interested in a lot of what Jerry had to say, and since this is my last letter to you, I'll just go ahead and say that. There were days where I felt you two were picking up a frequency like a dog whistle that I just wasn't able to hear. Of course, you might just have a great gift for empathy, but then I'd have to ask where was this gift when Jerry was trying to have me committed to the attic like that woman in *Jane Eyre* who set everything on fire.

I have to admit I was curious about you and your life, especially after I met your kid and saw your room, and what I observed undermined my confidence in what you might or might not know. I mean, those enormous ornate cornices you all chose in your bedroom I can overlook. That is *my* business after all, and a lot of people make the unfortunate mistakes you did. Yellow really is a hard color to pick and work with. Any artist will tell you that. But my advice would be to go in there and start from scratch. That overhead light looks like something Liberace might've had in the bathroom.

I think it would help in your job if you had a chart of sorts that told people how they *should* feel. This is a normal range of jealousy and here is where you went off the deep end. Here is true compassion and concern and this is malicious and calculated. Like that's what I'd say about Jerry putting me on the prayer list at his new church. People keep leaving fruit on my steps and I keep driving over to Jerry's house and throwing it through the window. "Stop praying for me!" I said, and he said, "I can pray for whomever I want." He said he would continue to pray for those like me—the sick and deranged. I didn't say what was on my unbrushed tongue, which shows how far I have come from the anger of it all. I am evolving each and every day. That's what I told Jerry when he sighed and stared to the heavens and mumbled something on my behalf. Instead of putting a foot in his face as I desired, I just told how at *my* church, my own personal testimony had inspired many. How I told I was born into chaos—a swirl of dust and stacked newspapers and old plastic-lined drapes that had not been opened in years—how my parents had sex that one time and then I was on my own tidying up when no one was looking and reading house magazines about decluttering and complimentary colors. "I am so evolved," I told Jerry, "I never had wisdom teeth. I have an innate sense to get rid of what I don't need."

So, DO YOU EVER wonder what happened to us? Good old Jerry and Hannah. We went to a mediator after you, and we're still dealing with the lawyers, the kids going back and forth every week like little ping-pong balls. It's all complicated. I know you see it all the time, enough that perhaps you can predict the ending to those like us, but aren't you ever curious or is it just part of the job, part of the day, like you're just one of many stops on the underground railroad? Or maybe not, since I can't imagine a slave choosing to go back or to just sit and talk indefinitely. *Emancipation* was a word on my mind before I even knew it was there.

Many of our problems began—as you should remember—when Jerry wanted to buy a house in town known as the murder-suicide house because he knew we could get it for a song. He was also putting in a bid on several divorce houses for the same reason. He doesn't believe in the supernatural elements the way that I do, unless, of course, it's biblical. He believes that Abraham heard a voice say that he should take his fully grown son and kill him on a mountaintop and that Moses heard and took dictation for the world, but he doesn't believe that I sometimes hear a little voice say *don't go there* like I might be in an Alfred Hitchcock movie heading toward the basement. He doesn't feel the wood of the floors straining to tell what really happened the way I do. Now I did not say that in therapy because it was during all that time he wanted to have me diagnosed as someone hearing voices. I had a hard time arguing the difference between literal and figurative. "A deal is a deal," he always said, even when I pointed out it wasn't if you didn't want it to begin with. Interior design is my business, a whole little popular business that centers around a kind of recycled cottage look, and he was trying to move me into a huge modern ant farm with black marble floors where on one unfortunate night an angry woman done wrong popped a bottle on the head of her husband and instead of running, as most people would do, killed herself with a knife right on top of him.

"No stains," Jerry said. "Very Romeo and Juliet. Fifty thousand less than that rundown bungalow you love."

I was holding a big bottle of Perrier and I gave a look that let him know he was on my last nerve, so he moved on to the divorce house, which was across the street.

"All glass, brand new, nothing to fix," he said.

"Nothing but the marriage," I said, but he didn't seem to hear. If it's not on the Mensa quiz, it might not be worth his attention.

"Can't throw stones if you live here," the Realtor said, but I told her that Jerry could because he was without sin.

AND SPEAKING OF HOUSES. Yours is palatial. A *special buyer* is what the Realtors will tell you that you need when you decide to sell and you won't know if that's a compliment or like when a handicapped person is being described. Were you planning a compound or what? A school? Did you think you'd have six kids and then change your mind when that one took up the habit of putting safety pins in her neck? When Jerry told how I have an awful sense of direction, that is actually true, and your house is so big it's easy to get all turned around.

"The Crazy Pit is that way," this kid said to me. Crazy Pit. And I smelled some serious reefer action, but of course I didn't tell you that your daughter was stoned and sad looking because then you would've known that I went the wrong way and saw your king-size bed and those unfortunate drapes and a big stack of strewn papers in the corner. I really wanted better for you in that moment. And I really wanted better for your daughter. You owe her. As soon as they arrive, we owe them. They didn't ask to be here. If we chose to have them, then we *made* them live; we made them come on out and be with the likes of us. We owe them big time.

IF I HAD YOUR JOB, I might ask a person: *If there was a nuclear disaster and you had to live out those final painful days just stretched out somewhere thinking about your life—This is who I am. This is what I love. This is what I believe.—who do you want hearing your whispers?* Or perhaps better: *Who do you trust to hear your whispers? Whose breath do you want mingled with your own? Whose flesh still warm beside you?*

I once heard a preacher discuss the miracles of Jesus in a way that made total sense to me. He said that science could explain the act but that what was a miracle was the timing. And every now and then during that period of time we were seeing you, I would wake in the middle of the night to an old feeling, a sad feeling. Some dream had transported me back to when I could feel. And I could remember what *hope* felt like. Not happiness necessarily, but hope, and there's a kind of natural happiness that grows out of hope, a kind of longing and imagining of what might be. You can take this old rundown house and make it look good. Paint and fabric and the right lightbulbs. Soften the angles, open the windows.

You know, back when I was so miserable, I read true crime all the time, the grizzlier the better, and I wondered, *What is wrong with me?* But I needed to reassure myself about where I was. At least I wasn't married to a serial killer. At least he didn't make me pretend to be dead or a young boy when having sex. Those aren't bodies stacked up out there in his tool shed but little Tupperware containers with sorted screws and nails. The fascination with someone else's reality is a total escape (this is where I think you might come in). We look at a bad situation and say, "Whew," or we laugh/judge/ridicule. We want confessions—car wrecks, true crime, divorce battles, someone's nervous breakdown. Who is the fattest person in the family? But what kind of life is that, if you have to spend all your time filling up on all the awful stuff that is *not* your life? I had just ordered video biographies on John Wayne Gacy (sicko clown) and Jeffrey Dahmer (cannibal) when I caught a glimpse of myself in your bathroom mirror and thought, *Oh my God.* And that is when I had to slam on the brakes. I slammed on brakes, and with it the world crashed, and with the wreckage

I heard silence, and with the silence I heard my own voice. I had been screaming all the while. For years I had been screaming. It was just like in *Horton Hears a Who!* and that realization also made me see how selfish all this divorce/religion/self-analysis can be—I had not read to my children or just sat and watched their television programs with them in weeks. I had not stretched out beside them and rubbed their backs, whispered about all the good things that will happen in their lives until they fell asleep. I had not done a thing to my hair in months and I had worn the same jeans for a week straight, the same ones I had let my scarecrow wear the whole summer before. I was a mess.

Remember how I finally ended our time with you? Remember how I made a big confession that I had fucked the plumber who stopped by to make a few repairs? Well, the truth is I didn't do that at all. That's the story you hear all the time, kind of like the banker and his secretary, the professor and his student. The carpenter, electrician, plumber. The butcher and the baker and the candlestick maker. That is a cliché right out of porn central. Bored wife wanders around the house all day wearing little to nothing and fucks whatever passes by. And you all believed it. Now *that* was *offensive* to me. I may be a lot of things but cliché is not one of them. And of course Jerry didn't really believe it but jumped on it like a dog on a bone because then he could accuse me of something specific. Alienation of affection.

Boo hoo. And when he threatened to let it affect the decision about the kids and how we would divide household goods, I just started singing "(I'm) a Boy Watcher," and we agreed to disagree and call it a truce.

THOUGH WE NEVER discussed it, I think deep down Jerry must know that I am too loyal a person to have screwed the plumber—loyal to the kids, loyal to my own moral code, and loyal to my own sense of aesthetics (no offense to the plumber, of course, but *not* my taste at all). No, my biggest betrayal to Jerry is that I quit trying. When I finally found my own voice, I realized there was nothing else I wanted to say to him. I stopped talking, nothing feeding nothing until nothing was huge and nothing begot nothing. Feeling nothing is not good, but it's where a lot of people stop and stay. The nothingness is so delusional and numbing. It's like stretching out in the snow and taking a little nap, and the comfort of discomfort is a scary thing. The lull into nothingness should be feared by all. Your daughter had a look of nothing that day, and I keep hoping she's better, that something in this world woke her back up. And I hope that as you read this letter you are actually able to identify me, to place me among the assembly line of broken parts and broken hearts that pass through your business. I hope you are able to remember how I often had to pee at the most unlikely (boring) times and how you have always wished that you had gotten my grandmother's pound cake recipe I described so well one day when you asked me to talk about something I was proud of, or that you wish you had gotten my advice on your entryway, which—if asked—would be to get rid of some of those primitive masks and weaponry. I know you are proud of all those times you went to Asian and African places but I just have to tell you, it's depressing. Maybe I got speared and boiled in a pot in some past life, I don't know, but those things give me the creeps. I'm afraid you'll come out there one day and find a client speared right there in the hallway with what came off your wall and her husband just a trail of exhaust in the distance and then you'll never sell this place. But what I'm most afraid of is that you'll make it too easy for people to come there and stay, get comfortable with the little games and the burden of trying to fix something that just can't be fixed. I hope you will remember that whatever I was, I was not apathetic. Bored? Oh dear God, yes, I was bored much of the time, but whenever I said I was bored or lonely or tired, it was my own voice saying it. I heard a voice that said, *Feel something.* And so I did, and I continue to. I wish you peace and love, Dr. Love. I wish you a happy daughter and a smooth-running vehicle and better décor. I thank you for the time you have spent reading me free of charge.

Sincerely,

Hannah from three suburbs over

PS: Enclosed is a photo of me and my kids at Disney World right after we rode Space Mountain, which is why the little one looks kind of scared. She barely made it up to the height mark that will let you ride. It was so much fun we went as many times as we could and even after screaming and carrying on and getting slung back and forth, I am proud to say that I no longer look one bit like shit on a stick.

DRIVING TO THE MOON

"WHAT I REALLY hate about major disasters," Billy was fond of saying, "is how they take away from all the smaller disasters, none of them any less disastrous." He had more or less introduced himself that way to Sarah and the whole small town of Fulton, North Carolina, in the fall of 1974 when he showed up late for football season their senior year. He'd continued through the years to connect with her at odd times with that line. He had called on 9/11 in fact, as the twin towers crumbled again and again on the television while Sarah waited for the school bus to bring her sons home. Until that day in 2001, the disaster associated with September 11 was the plane crash in 1974 of a domestic flight from Charleston to Chicago that claimed the lives of his parents and older sister. Billy went from being a prep school kid, son of a surgeon, to being the orphaned grandson of an old tobacco farmer in eastern North Carolina. The plane's black box revealed that the crew members were talking and laughing too much—talking about politics and used cars, telling jokes—and as a result the Sterile Cockpit Rule came into being. Billy said the last thing you want to be is part of a lesson about how *not* to die. Studies were also done on how much more severe the burns were on those dressed in polyester, prompting his classic line about how his mother wouldn't have been caught dead in polyester. She was in gabardine. Armani. The suit she got his dad to buy for her the year before with the promise it would last her a lifetime.

The information about the crash preceded Billy's arrival, but it was clear that he would have had all the attention anyway—he was one of those boys "too handsome and smart for his own good," the principal was overheard saying when Billy got sent to the office for refusing to stand for the Pledge of Allegiance. The fact that he was an orphan just made everyone want him more. The boys wanted to *be* him or at least to befriend him, and the girls wanted to be *with* him, to be the one who could bring some happiness back into his life. For better or worse, Sarah was right in there with the best of them and had remained so through thirty-odd years of a friendship that had cycled through puppy love and youthful lust, being a couple and then not, years of anger and then regret, and finally back around to some claim on that strong affection they knew in the beginning.

"THERE'S ALWAYS A most popular dead person," he called to say when the *Challenger* exploded. "It really pisses me off, too. So unfair." Sarah had been dating her future husband for only a few months and he was there with her, half dressed and a little impatient that she had stopped to answer the phone. They had already watched the explosion many times over, had already spoken so sadly about Christa McAuliffe—ordinary schoolteacher on a mission—the dream of a lifetime. "Hey, are you there?" This was the first time she had actually heard his voice since their own blowup at the end of the six months they lived together at the beach. The decision to share space came during a long winter day while watching the rescue attempts of Flight 90 that went down in the Potomac. Billy had said he couldn't stop watching, that he kept hoping the guy who passed the rescue line to others so many times would wise up the next time it played and get selfish, choose to save his own neck. He then said he could get used to not being alone and they went on from there.

Four years had passed, days on end when she assumed he would do the right thing and at least call or respond to her angry messages and letters. Instead he had taken off and gone to Alaska for a while. Then he was somewhere way up in the mountains of Tennessee. She had gotten a postcard in the summer of 1985 on the heels of the catastrophic Air India and Japan Airlines flights.

His scrawled note said, "Shitty summer for travelers. Thinking of you."

"Sarah?" he said again, the *Challenger* blowing up in slow motion on the screen.

"Yes. I'm here."

"Got a husband? A boyfriend?"

"Yes."

"Which?" He laughed and in the background she could hear bottles clanking and music playing. Out her window, the winter trees were as stripped bare as she felt in the moment, their lean rattling limbs more comforting than the arms opening to her from across the room, a finger beckoning her to hang up the phone.

"The second."

"What's it to you? That's what you want to say, isn't it." She could tell he had been drinking. "If the boyfriend wasn't right there breathing down your neck, you would say that, too." He laughed again. "What's it to you, asshole? I don't know anybody on the *Challenger*. I don't give a shit about you."

But she knew that he knew better than that.

HE CALLED WHEN 183 people died in a crash in Poland and then 290 more on Iran Air. He called right after the explosion over Lockerbie and asked her to sit quietly with him while they timed what those thrown from the plane at 31,000 feet had lived through. He told her how it was likely during that two-minute fall that passengers, still strapped in their seats, woke while passing through lower altitudes—nightmare to end all nightmares. Afterwards the rescue team found one young man they were fairly certain was still alive on impact. There was a mother holding her baby, a couple holding hands. "I bet my parents were holding hands when they went down," he said. "I bet my dad was saying all the right things." Sarah was holding her infant son at the time, nursing him in her darkened bedroom; she could see the Christmas tree lit and glowing down the hall, where her husband was building a fire and wrapping gifts.

He was a voice through the wire, a voice in her head, even as she passed through major milestone moments: her second son born, a graduate degree, father dying, new job. There was a progression of houses, moves for more bedrooms, then a bigger yard, better schools, and then just because it was something she and her husband might enjoy doing, something new, something different. There were clubs and dinner parties and Neighborhood Watch meetings. Books read and vacations taken, anniversaries celebrated with dinner out and the perfect gifts chosen. Still, she thought of Billy often. He sent the occasional postcard from exotic places, and then she spent days wondering why *then*, what was going on in life that made him stop and think of her *then*, take the time to write. He had married several times, moved around with different jobs, but he was always successful, and who knew if it was due to the magic orphan card he had learned to play so well or just great survival techniques. The calls from Billy marked her life like little train stations, dim hamlets that she moved toward, sensing they would be there when she least expected, the glow she would look over her shoulder to glimpse for miles and miles in the distance.

THE CALL TO COME tell him good-bye was not a surprise. Sarah had heard a month before that he'd gotten a bad diagnosis, and though they were too young to be dying, barely fifty, she seemed to know more and more people heading that way. She might have gotten by with cards and a phone call, the occasional "remember when" letter, had he not called her himself to request her presence at his going-away party. When he finished the well-rehearsed invitation, he added, "Besides, you still have some of my albums you never returned. Isn't that the classic cliché? I say, 'You have my *White Album*, Pure Prairie League, and the Clapton with "I Shot the Sheriff,"' and then you say something like, 'But they're mine. I used my paycheck from IHOP.'"

The confusing thing was that he must have known what he was doing in the moment, the manipulation of material, or else it was a weird subconscious moment of guilt, because she *did* buy that particular Pure Prairie League album with her waitressing money because he loved that song "Amie." What she hadn't known was how he was screwing someone named Amie at the time. Those six months together in 1982 had been the happiest time she had known and might have been the beginning of the rest of their lives but instead—and unfortunately, she had always thought—was abruptly ended when she discovered someone else's underwear when changing the sheets.

"I couldn't help it," he said. "I'm a guy."

"A guy," she repeated. "Your dad the god of surgeons was a guy. Did he ever do that to your perfect saintly mother or were they always sitting and holding hands and thinking about you?"

"That is the most hurtful thing you have ever said." He was holding the underwear in his hand, a flesh-colored strip of silk. "You're not perfect either."

"You're a *disaster*," she said when she left, cramming everything she could into that Karmann Ghia so she wouldn't have to come back and risk finding him with someone else. "You've always been a disaster."

When he paused on the phone, she could hear his breathing and all kinds of hospital noise. "Remember how we ate off of campware all the time?" he asked.

"Yes."

"And how the only thing you ever cooked was that fluorescent sweet-and-sour chicken with those Maraschino cherries?"

"Yes."

"I think it was the combination of those two things that got me. Red dye and aluminum."

"Ha ha."

"Look, I get sprung tomorrow," he said. "And then it's just a matter of time, so don't wait too long. Don't wait like when I begged you to come to Santa Fe."

"I was married then and so were you."

"I was only half-married."

She looked down at her calendar as he talked. Her youngest son had varsity soccer tryouts and the oldest, a sophomore at Clemson, had planned to come home for the weekend. Her husband had to lecture out of town. The library where she worked in special collections was under construction and she had promised to work extra hours to get everything organized. In a movie, life would stop for such an event, but it doesn't happen in reality. People bury spouses and go right back to work. Disasters happen and people pay their bills and go to the grocery store. In her mind she imagined the drive—just under three hours—she could get up early and make a day of it; she could rearrange a couple of things and be back in plenty of time to take the kids out to dinner and wash all the laundry her son would bring home from college.

In a letter to Billy over a year ago she had written that she still had the old Karmann Ghia she had in high school, that her husband had recently gone to great pains to get it running again in hopes that their youngest might drive it. She was aware of how she didn't use her husband's name when speaking to Billy. She never had and he likewise had kept his women blank and unspecific. Now he was asking her to drive the distance to see him. "That's what I want for my going-away present," he said. Someone there was telling him he needed to hang up. "If you don't come take me for a ride in that car, I'll die."

SARAH GOT THE Karmann Ghia in 1975, the same year she met Billy, and the two events have remained entwined in her memory. She was a senior in high school, almost eighteen. She had smiled at him several times in passing at school before actually being introduced, and each time her heart had pounded in a way that she felt must be visible there under the bumpy bra and Elton John T-shirt she almost always wore to practice. She wasn't sure which was more exciting: the new boy in town or the new used car parked in the school lot waiting for her and one lucky friend to cruise along with the top down and radio playing.

Five feet ten inches of good-looking orphaned boy or a thousand-plus pounds of shiny green metal? Four in the floor or pale blue eyes like a Weimaraner? When she told him—while they lived together as a couple—that she had often confused her excitement for him with that of her car, he had said that made perfect sense. "We've both been used," he said. "And we both run hot." She wanted to ask who had used him. She wanted to be the one who would make everything okay. It would be years before she realized what a dangerous position it was to be a self-appointed missionary even to those in need. He said simply that life had used him, and he shook his head in a somber disillusioned way. "But," he added, "the good thing about when your family is dead is you're not afraid. Like all those times you worry that something will happen to them. Done, over. And you don't have to worry about them worrying. Can't disappoint what's not there. And holidays are so cheap and easy."

"You can shift *my* stick," he said on numerous occasions. His silly retorts led to an even sillier passion. He had confessed to her his great love for the music his mother had listened to—Frank Sinatra, Bobby Darin, and lots of Broadway selections. This was what was stacked on the turntable ready to play every night while his mom sipped a glass of wine and cooked dinner. He still had her turntable just that way, and though he listened often, he never changed the order. He described her in a way that made her sound like Mary Tyler Moore or Audrey Hepburn in black fitted slacks and ballet-style shoes. A beautiful and stylish woman who never raised her voice and was always there when he needed her.

Revealing his love for these old songs, a detail so out of character with the way he presented himself, was what he gave her in return after badgering her to confess that she was still a virgin, that she had not even engaged in what allowed girls to maintain "technical virginity." The swap of information hardly seemed fair as he first expressed great sympathy for her boyfriend before consoling and telling her that she was right to wait for the perfect time. His hand lingered longer than it needed to on her shoulder, fingers dropped and stroking the skin just above her right breast. She knew that if she had turned the slightest bit, he would have kissed her and that hand would have gone God knows where, so she decided to play a card back at him, to get him to share a secret. He laughed, told how his mother sang things like "Mack the Knife" for a lullaby, how one of his best memories was of her doing what they called the shark face—showing her pearly white teeth. Chubby Checker was another favorite. He said the only time he ever saw his dad relax was after a couple of drinks when his mom convinced him to dance.

Ironically, his best memories of his dad involved flying—first as a toddler lifted up high and then later when he and his sister were instructed to get down in the floorboard of their Country Squire wagon barreling down the interstate and close their eyes while their father narrated from the cockpit all that was happening. The clear runway, the increasing speed, then his dad would say "lift off," and the sensation was so real that when Billy opened his eyes and looked up, all he could see out the windows were stars. Billy drove through the backroads and directed Sarah to do what he had done as a kid, to close her eyes and pretend to be flying. They rode Highway 211 to the beach—flat miles of swamp and stripped timber. They often went miles without seeing another car, past the homemade-ice-cream shop and farm stands, and past Lockwoods Folly, an area named for a man who once built a big beautiful ship and then had no way to get it to the ocean.

OVER THE YEARS, Sarah thought of Billy with any disaster that involved planes. She had called once only the year before when a small private plane went down near the coast, hesitating before leaving the simple message "Thinking of you." There was a time when she would have simply hung up, but technology had changed that. A person could no longer be anonymous, no longer reach out and hear the voice and breath of someone she loved without being discovered. Before caller ID she had called him many times that way, lying to herself and rationalizing as soon as she hung up, then remembering to get the bill in case her husband scanned the long-distance calls. The fact that she hid and protected her impulses was something she didn't fully understand and couldn't afford to analyze.

"Disasters," Billy once said. "It's my hobby." He said that he watched and kept up with the crashes, the tallies, the whole new civilization sprung, those like him, orphaned by a plane crash. "And you think my tribe is something," he said. "You ought to count up the car-accident people. The murders. The suicide people."

"I have an idea," he said not long after they met. "Let's drive to the moon." At the time, the car was only two years old and had barely 7,000 miles. It had been a toy her father's friend purchased when he turned forty only to discover that he was way too large for it and decided to go with a Trans Am instead.

"How many miles on it?" Billy asked, and she told him.

"So only 231,857 miles to go."

And then it began, the constant tallying of miles as she drove them everywhere. It was something they kept to themselves. Her boyfriend was off in college, faithfully writing letters and assuring her that she was worth waiting for, and Billy had a rotating harem that included a married woman who was twenty-nine. He was the kind of boy always running from places, always "zipping trou," as he called it, always saved by the skin of his teeth. When they were riding around, wind whipping their hair, they sang things like "Beyond the Sea" or "*Drive* Me to the Moon." Thirty-two years and many miles later, the odometer read 238,514.

THREE HUNDRED AND forty-three miles to go. If it didn't break down, the trip to tell Billy good-bye would bring the car within miles of its goal. This was a meeting she had known would eventually happen, just not this way. She knew he was married and had been twice before this latest one. He wasn't at their tenth high school reunion (he was somewhere in Alaska) or their fifteenth (somewhere in Europe), which had left her filled with loss even though her own husband was there beside her. She would go stretches without thinking of Billy, but as soon as she hit the city limits, he was *all* she could think about. She was pulled with a kind of gravitational force to ride by and see all the familiar places.

She passed his house, the window he climbed out of, the place on the interstate where they met. She recalled the way they slipped through the woods, then an old corn field, across the service road, and finally up the concrete ramp of the overpass. It wasn't filthy then, no graffiti, just a clean concrete ledge up under the bridge where they could sit and watch the cars passing. It was wide enough they could even stretch out side by side. Now when driving anywhere, Sarah is aware of the homeless people bedded beneath the bridges, shopping carts filled with their belongings. Where were the homeless back then? She remembered only the sound of cars and trucks passing, comforting like the roll of the ocean. She and Billy crept up the concrete slant below the bridge and crouched there, his blue jean jacket around her shoulders. He said he could teach her things if she wanted. His offer came with a mischievous smile. "You know, so you won't be nervous when you do decide to be with *him*." And so he taught her everything she might ever need to know. *Almost*, he might say, *but we might need to practice a little bit more. Lighter on the teeth, heavy on the lyrics*. He suggested she sing something from *Camelot*—"If Ever I Would Leave You" or "The Lusty Month of May."

At the twenty-fifth reunion, he arrived with the

much younger woman who would be his third wife. Billy and Sarah circled each other carefully and cordially for two hours before finally—too many drinks later—she found herself with him on the dance floor, slightly dizzy from the drinks but mainly dizzy because of the song, "Stairway to Heaven," which was the way every high school dance had ended. It made her feel as if she had never left his side, never left home, never had a life other than this one. "Still driving to the moon?" he whispered, and her heart pounded just as it had years before, even as her husband sat talking to a group of her classmates, even as her sons, then eleven and six, watched television in her childhood home, where her mother now lived alone.

"I'm still about sixty thousand miles away," she said and leaned in as close as she could. She half expected to feel him pressed against her as had always happened at every dance, forcing them to dash outside to some dark corner or the tiny enclosure of her car. She had to keep reminding herself where she was in time. The way he looked at her let her know he had read her mind. "Not you," he whispered. "Blood-pressure medicine."

"It's not my primary car, always has been prone to breakdowns, so the process is a little slower."

"Isn't everything?" He laughed and pressed closer, then still closer, this time more like old times. "I'm not dead yet," he breathed. "It just took a moon day is all. Fourteen times what it used to be."

She laughed, forgetting where they were. "I always think of you when it's full," he said. "I'm probably the only person on the planet disappointed by a full moon—like Pavlov's dog well trained." The full moon was their old buzzword for when she was having her period. Full moon every twenty-nine and a half days.

"Still dependable as clockwork," she said. "I've decided not to go through the change. I've decided to stay young."

"Good information for a guy to have," he said as they moved slowly over the dance floor, occasionally bumping into people they hadn't seen in twenty-five years. They held on a little longer, even as the last notes played and people moved from the floor. "I'm not dead and you're still young."

Later she would think how crazy it had been that they had had such a conversation there on the dance floor with their spouses and classmates scattered about in grown-up attire telling grown-up tales about their occupations and children. They talked about periods and erections and laughed about it all as if they were seventeen. She had watched Billy (or Bill as he was now known) the whole night, where he was, who he was talking to, the eye contact as powerful as those early memories of him. And when they left to go home, she took the keys from her husband though she had probably had more to drink than he had and she cranked his BMW, shifted into reverse and then back into drive, and all but flew toward the familiar interstate that cut through her hometown. Barely visible through the sunroof was a new moon—slivered crescent—that thrilled her with the thought of what might happen next. But thirty-six hours later she was firmly rooted back in her life, and Billy remained the distant fantasy he had always been.

SHE WIPED DOWN the car and stepped back to take a look: CARTER/MONDALE and the GRATEFUL DEAD stickers. In later years she drove it to a Dixie Chicks concert with a girlfriend in the midst of a bad divorce and added EARL'S IN THE TRUNK. Parking stickers from all the places she had lived and worked. A single life. A young married life. She got in and leaned back, breathed in the smell of the hard cracked leather, stale cigarette smoke still lingering, an old Bonne Bell lip gloss melted in the cup holder where there had always been a can of Tab.

When she called back to say she would definitely be there, he said: "I knew my dying would get your attention." He paused. "If only you'd responded sooner I might not have to die at all."

"You've been dying since I met you thirty years ago."

"But now it's real."

"We're all dying."

"But not with an estimated time of departure," he sighed. "And I want all my women gathered for the big show like the big stars, you know. Henry Fonda, Dean Martin, Johnny Carson. Didn't they have their women all there in a harem to say good-bye?"

pause. "Like Yul Brynner in *The King and I*."

BILLY WAS SITTING on the front steps when she pulled into his drive. His house was a small white Colonial with an assortment of Little Tikes structures in the side yard—a green plastic turtle and a yellow-and-red slide. Her sons had had those same toys. The wife waved from the front window, then leaned out the door to blow him a kiss, to wave a hello and thanks to Sarah while holding the hand of the curly-haired boy who was trying to follow his dad.

"Have fun," she called, and Billy told her it was a given, and then when she was back in the house he turned to Sarah. "Can't believe you still have this car," he said and climbed into the passenger seat. "Smells the same, feels the same." He closed his eyes, giving her time to study how much he had changed. "Maybe if we drive it in reverse we can go back in time."

"Worth a try." She started the car and backed up a few feet.

"Do you believe in life beyond?" He opened his eyes then and looked at her.

"I want to."

"Not an answer. Everyone wants to." They drove in silence to the highway, and then as soon as she sped up to enter traffic and the wind noise filled the small car with a hum, he started talking. "Fate fucked me over," he began. He explained that he was supposed to be born much earlier, how if he had been born in the late 1920s then he would be just right. A teen in the '40s, just missing World War II, and then all settled in the '50s with a kind of briefcase job and picket fence bungalow. In the '60s he'd have been protesting and driving his son to Canada, '70s dressing like Bob Newhart, greedy in the '80s, doing yoga and Kabbalah in the '90s, a spokesman for the new century. "I probably would've buried a few wives," he said, "women tired and worn out from serving me, and I'd be looking for a replacement—the latest model or version or edition, depending on what we're comparing her to. I bet I could get one right this minute, some good-looking young thing to do a few weeks hospice care for all of my money."

"You wore out a lot of women in this life, they just didn't die."

"Is that the voice of experience?" He laughed and propped a bare foot up on the dash, the thin white scar on his anklebone visible. He once called that scar his sister proof, the proof that once upon a time he had her, and then he told Sarah how his foot got caught in his sister's bicycle spokes when she let him ride on the back fender.

"Where are we now?" he asked.

"Clarkton."

"How far to the moon?"

"Only about two hundred more miles."

"How about the beach?"

"Five miles." She slowed. "Should you call home?"

"No service." He slumped and closed his eyes. "Didn't you date a guy named Clark? Didn't you do something really obnoxious?"

"Called him Kent all night."

He laughed. "Yeah, you were really pissed. You really wanted to be with me that night, didn't you? And you said something to him about a phone booth."

"I said why didn't he jump into one and become someone super?"

"That's right," he said. "I was super. And you wanted super." He shook his head, slapped a hand on her shoulder and then kept it there, kneading slowly. "Do you remember that song 'Seasons in the Sun'?"

"Yes."

"How I made fun of it? And made fun of anybody who liked it?"

"Yes."

"Hokey sentiment. I still think it sucks."

"Me too."

"K-tel presents *Songs that Suck.* You want good-bye? *Man of La Mancha,* there's good-bye. So much of what's out there just sucks, don't you think?"

"Yes."

"I think cancer sucks."

"Me too."

"Losing people sucks."

"Yeah."

"That wasn't convincing. What about losing me all those years ago?"

"Sucked."

"But was it right?"

"Who knows?"

"I will soon. They'll tell me at the gate. They'll say, list all your mistakes on earth, and I'll tell how I wish I had told my mom how good she smelled, how I could find her right now in a thick dark cave like a bat. I once dated a girl for that smell and it took me forever to figure out why I liked being with her. The only thing she had going for her was a bottle of Halston cologne."

"If I'd only known."

"You didn't need it. Had your own good smell." He took her hand from the wheel, sniffed, and then kissed her wrist. "But you did interrupt me the way you've always done. It's rude and it pisses me off."

She zipped her lips and then held up her middle finger, beckoned that he continue.

"Well, then I'll say I made a mistake when I missed a throw to third that would have won my sixth-grade Little League championship, and that I was sorry I picked on Howie Thompkins, bleeding chicken of the neighborhood I grew up in who later took himself out. I shouldn't have gone swimming the afternoon my grandfather was dying; everybody told me I needed to stick around and I didn't. I told my kids, in fact, 'No swimming till I'm gone.' It's a really long shitty list and I'm pretty sure losing you is on it." He paused. "Aren't you going to say something?"

"Only when you're all finished. Don't want to interrupt."

"All done. I ended by saying I was pretty sure losing you was way up on the list of shitty things I've done."

"Every woman's fantasy. So is this what you're doing? Last words for everyone like party favors? Do you tell your kids that you have mammoth amounts of money stashed away for them? Ponies and cars for future grandkids?"

He didn't laugh but stared straight ahead, the skin of his neck pale and goosefleshed. "Do you think I did something to bring this on? Is it because I'm such an asshole?"

"You're not an asshole."

"What am I?"

"Corny, immature, unfaithful."

"The truth comes out." He moved his hand to her neck and massaged as he talked. "Remember that story about Brother Moon and Sister Sun, the great incest story about eclipses? Remember how I wanted us to act it out for science class?"

"I remember well. And it's not *just* an incest story. It's a rape story, too."

"Kinda sexy."

"Kinda creepy. It ends with her doing something really awful like mutilating herself."

"Remember making those boxes to see the eclipse?" he asked.

"Peep boxes."

"They said we'd go blind if we looked."

"That's what I was told would happen if I jerked off."

"So you made me do it for you."

"Made?"

"Yeah."

"Can I make you again?" Nothing.

"Would you believe that's the morphine talking?"

"Yes, I would."

"Yes, you would oblige me or yes, you would believe?"

When she didn't answer, he pushed her shoulder, nudged until she laughed with him.

"You know," he said. "This is the best day ever. Who knew I'd have to be dying to get it." He closed his eyes again, hand limp on her shoulder. She wanted him to be faking, to pick this time to tell her it was all an elaborate joke, that here in his fifties he had figured out illness would be a great way to get women.

"If you weren't . . ." she paused.

"Circling the drain? Knock-knock-knockin' on heaven's door? Croaking?"

"Yeah all that. If you weren't, I'd— "

"Kill me?"

"Slap you."

"Do you ever wonder why there aren't more apocalyptic acts performed by cancer troops? You're dying anyway, can't go to prison. Hell, in our system you wouldn't even live to have a hearing . . ."

"The good side of man."

"I forget there is one."

"Everyone has a good side."

"And a dark one. Think of it—the cancer mafia—skinny people dragging IVs. Go ahead, make my day. You talking to me? *Hasta la vista,* baby."

THEY WERE PASSING a small churchyard, and the stark white of the headstones was a shock to the soft green background. Already she could see the skeletal structure of his face. His plan long ago was cremation, some of which was to be scattered around the crash site of his family, but when his grandfather died, he had said that he couldn't let go of the old guy's body so easily.

She pulled off the highway and back toward his neighborhood. The closer they got, odometer creeping, the quieter he was. He fiddled with the old radio knob, getting only static.

"I hope we haven't been gone too long," she said.

"I hope *you* haven't been gone too long," he said. "Does your husband know we're meeting like this?"

"Yes," she lied, though a part of her wanted to tell the truth, to tell how her husband was jealous of him and always had been. How at the height of one argument he had said, "But you would leave me for Billy," the name bitter on his tongue, and she had not stepped forward to assure him that she wouldn't. She had never let go of the idea that someday they *would* have a future. Even now, she couldn't stop believing. Her husband's greatest rival was disappearing before her very eyes.

In front of his house, cars lined the curb. His kids were outside in the sandbox with a young girl who was being paid to watch them for awhile. They both wore cowboy hats and carried small plastic rifles. The girl had on pink boots and purple shorts.

"People are coming and praying. Please, let's keep driving. Remember *Thelma and Louise*? You loved that movie. Let's do it! We can drive off the overpass."

"I didn't like the end."

"You did at the time, and if you were them you'd know there's no other choice—the ultimate sacrifice."

"Been there."

"You talking 'bout me?"

"Yes, Narcissus, I am." Now Sarah felt anxious to get him back inside, and then to get herself home and to the grocery store. In all her haste she had forgotten to feed the dog and imagined him sitting there at the back door confused and feeling abandoned. She had not told anyone where she was. She had turned off her phone hours ago. His wife came out to the car and stood waiting for him to get out. She held his arm and then motioned for Sarah to join her, the two of them helping him in where he collapsed in his chair. He looked like an old man wearing Billy's eyes.

"You know what I've always fantasized about?" He looked back and forth between the two of them, his life split like a walnut shell. His wife laughed and turned to the door to greet yet another person bringing in a dish of something.

"The buzzards are swooping in," he whispered. "Say nice things. Lie to my children." But as he spoke, he touched the crystals, the tea cup, the books on the table. "Somebody's been fucking with my feng shui," he said. "Don't go fucking with my chi, now. My yin and yang, especially my yang."

The wife returned in time to hear him and laughed. She was so tired she was ready to laugh at anything. She had had a holiday. An hour all alone and a glass of wine. The empty glass was on the mantel and there was music playing—not from Broadway—but pop music, oldies, the music of their generation, much of which he greeted with such disdain.

The wife asked Sarah to stay just another minute while she tried to get people to clear out so she could cook some dinner and get the kids settled. "My brother will be here soon," she said, seemingly avoiding Billy's eyes.

"She's afraid to leave me too long at a time," he whispered and then reached out and patted her on the bottom. She caught his hand and he held on tight, holding her near until she kissed the top of his head and then pulled away.

"That's right," she said and nudged his shoulder the same way he had done Sarah's in the car. "He misbehaves." She thanked Sarah and went back into the kitchen, where there were murmurs of conversation.

"You heard it. We got her permission," he said. "So what do you want to do?"

"You tell me." She sat in the chair right beside his, their arms close enough to touch.

"Well, I'm feeling too tired for sex," he said. "Maybe in a little bit." He fished in the basket beside his chair, where there were all kinds of other crystals and herb bundles and what looked like rosaries. "Bob?" He held up a DVD of *The Bob Newhart Show,* a program they had watched faithfully on Saturday nights in high school. "How about the one where Bob gets drunk and orders all that Chinese food?"

"Okay."

"And maybe this time he won't drink too much. Or maybe this time, Emily won't leave and go out of town." He was about to stand but she took the disc and walked across the room to the television. "Do you remember how when his other show ended, he woke up and was back in bed with Suzanne Pleshette in the first show like it was all a dream?"

"Yeah." She put the disc in and came back over beside him.

"I almost called you. I kept thinking how that might happen to us except that you'd probably still be pissed off about whatever that girl's name was."

"Her name was Amie, and I would have been." She hit play and the episode began.

"I never tuck in the sheet because of what happened. My wife wants to and I just can't do it." He grins and shakes his head. "I don't want history repeating itself." The familiar music began playing and then there was the skyline of Chicago, Bob Newhart racing to catch the train. "And history does repeat itself," he whispered. "Like how my kids are about to go through what I went through."

"They have their mom."

"I know, and I am so fucking jealous of that!" He took the control from her hand and hit pause just as Bob entered his office and closed the door. "How sick am I?" He put his hand to his chest, teeth clenched. "I keep thinking, *You lucky little shits to get to come home from the funeral and have a mother.*" He took a deep breath and then hit play, reached for her hand again and squeezed. They could see his kids and wife in the doorway, hear them talking. His wife told them she was making their dad's favorite dinner, and it occurred to Sarah that she had no idea what that might be. "Then he'll read to you," she said. There was the sound of a mixer, refrigerator opening and closing. The girl was singing a song Sarah recognized from *Sesame Street*, and on the screen Bob and Emily are interrupted by their neighbor, Howard, as they always are. Billy pointed to Bob's wide tie and laughed. In the kitchen, his daughter kicked her pink boot against the counter and demanded a snack. The boy dangled a bag of chips in the air, threw back his head and laughed.

Billy smiled, watching them, and then turned back to the television. "I don't want to go," he whispered.

"Then don't."

This was the conversation they might have had after everything blew up; it was what Sarah had always wished had been said. Billy was looking sleepy and said he just needed to rest his eyes for a minute.

"Promise you won't let Bob get drunk and screw up this time," he mumbled, the grip of his hand loosening as he dozed in and out.

"Okay." She heard someone at the door, his wife's brother. Bob was struggling to order the moo goo gai pan and having a terrible time speaking. Billy smiled during the slurred speech.

When it was time to leave, she pulled her hand from his and stood, debating whether or not to wake him to say good-bye. With the wife's encouragement, she leaned forward and hugged him.

"I wasn't really such a disaster, was I?" he asked.

"No, not really." She kissed his cheek quickly and then she was up and moving, in the car and moving forward, calling her husband to wish him a safe trip, calling home to leave a message for her sons, asking that they please feed the dog. She turned onto the highway, shifting gears and going faster and faster, under the overpass, and then full speed ahead, the pines a green blur off to the side, the odometer turning and turning as she flew right past the moon.

MAGIC WORDS

BECAUSE PAULA BLAKE is planning something secret, she feels she must account for her every move and action, overcompensating in her daily chores and whatever demands her husband and children make. *Of course I'll pick up the dry cleaning, drive the kids, swing by the drugstore.* This is where the murderer always screws up in a movie, way too accommodating, too much information. The guilty one always has trouble maintaining direct eye contact.

"Of course I will take you and your friend to the movies," she tells Erin in the late afternoon. "But do you think her mom can drive you home? I'm taking your brother to a sleepover, too." She is doing it again, talking too much.

"Where are *you* going?" Erin asks, mouth sullen and sarcastic as it has been since her thirteenth birthday two years ago.

"Out with a friend," Paula says, forcing herself to try and make eye contact. The rest of the story she has practiced for days, ready to roll. *She's someone I work with, someone going through a really hard time, someone brand new to the area, knows no one, really needs a friend.*

But her daughter never looks up from the glossy magazine spread before her, engrossed in yet another drama about a teen star lost to drugs and wild nights. Paula's husband doesn't even ask her new friend's name or where she moved from, yet the answer is poised and waiting on her tongue: *Tonya Matthews from Phoenix, Arizona.* But her husband is glued to his latest issue of *Our Domestic Wildlife*—his own newsletter to the neighborhood about various sightings of wild and possibly dangerous creatures: coyotes, raccoons, bats. Their voicemail is regularly filled with detailed sightings of funny-acting raccoons in daylight or reports of missing cats. Then there's the occasional giggling kid faking a deep voice to report a kangaroo or rhino. She married a reserved and responsible banker who now fancies himself a kind of watchdog Crocodile Dundee. They are both seeking interests beyond the safe perimeters of a lackluster marriage. His are all about threat and encroachment, being on the defense, and hers are about human contact, a craving for warmth, like one of the bats her husband fears might find its way into their attic.

Her silky legs burn as if shamed where she has slathered lavender body lotion whipped as light as something you might eat. And the new silk panties, bought earlier in the day, feel heavy around her hips. But it is not enough to thwart the thought of what is ahead of her, the consummation of all those notes and looks exchanged with the sales rep on the second floor during weeks at work, that one time in the stairwell—hard thrust of a kiss interrupted by the heavy door and footsteps two floors up—where the fantasized opportunity became enough of a reality to lead to this date. They have been careful and the paper trail is slight—unsigned suggestive notes with penciled times and places—all neatly rolled like tiny scrolls and saved in the toe of the heavy wool ski socks she has never worn back in the far corner of her underwear drawer, where heavier, far more substantial pairs of underwear than she is wearing cover the surface. It all feels as safe as it can be because he has a family, too. He has just as much to lose as she does.

And now she looks around to see the table filled with cartons of Chinese food and cereal boxes from the morning. The television blares from the other room. Her son is anxious to get to his sleepover; her daughter has painted her toenails, and the fumes of the purple enamel fill the air. Her husband is studying a map that shows the progression of killer bees up the coast. He speaks of them like hated relatives who are determined to drop in whether you want them or not. Their eventual arrival is as inevitable as all the other predicted disasters that will wreak havoc on human life.

"Where did you say you've got to go?" her husband asks. Her palms are sweating and she is glad she is wearing a turtleneck to hide the nervous splotches on her chest. She won't be wearing it later. She will slip it off in the darkness of the car after she takes Gregory to the sleepover and Erin and her friend to the cinema. Under the turtleneck she is wearing a thin silk camisole, also purchased that very afternoon at a pricey boutique she had never been in before, a place the size of a closet where individual lingerie items hang separately on the wall like art. A young girl, sleek, pierced, and polished, gave a cool nod of approval when she leaned in to look at the camisole. She finally chose the black one after debating between it and the peacock blue. Maybe she will get the blue next time, already hoping that this new part of her life will remain. Instead of the turtleneck, she will wear a loose cashmere cardigan that slides from one shoulder when she leans her head inquisitively. It will come off easily, leaving only the camisole between them in those first awkward seconds. She tilts her head as she has practiced, and with that thought all others disappear, and now she doesn't know what has even been asked of her. Her heart beats a little too fast. She once failed a polygraph test for this reason. She had never—would never—shoot heroin, but her pulse raced with the memory of someone she knew doing just that. Did she do drugs? The answer was no, but her mind took her elsewhere, to her panic when she saw her ride home from a high school party with his head thrown back and teeth gritted, arm tied off with a large rubber band, while a friend loomed overhead to inject him, one bloody needle already on the littered floor.

You can't afford to let your mind wander in a polygraph test or in life as now when once again she finds herself looking at her husband with no idea of what he has just said. Her ability to hold eye contact is waning, the light out the window, waning, but the desire that has built within all these weeks is determined to linger, flickering like a candle under weak labored breath. Somewhere, her husband says, between their house and the interstate, are several packs of coyotes, their little dens tucked away in brush and fallen trees. The coyote is a creature that often remains monogamous. The big bumbling mouthful of a word lingers there, a pause that lasts too long before he continues with his report. He heard the coyotes last night so this is a good time to get the newsletter out, a good time to remind people to bring their pets indoors. Dusk is when they come out, same as the bats, most likely rabid.

THE KIDS ARE DOING what they call creepy crawling. Their leader picked the term up from the book *Helter Skelter*. They slip in and out behind trees and bushes, surveying houses, peeping in windows, finding doors ajar or unlocked. Their leader is a badly wounded boy in need of wounding others, and so he frightens them, holds them enthralled with his stories of violence or murder. They might not believe all that he says but they believe enough to know he is capable of bad things. As frightening as it is to be with him, it is more frightening not to be, to be on the outside and thus a potential victim.

To the kids he looks tough with his piercings and tattoos, his mouth tight and drawn by a bitterness rarely seen on such a young face, some vicious word always coiled on his tongue and ready to strike those who least expect it, though he has to be careful when bagging groceries at Food Lion; he has been reprimanded twice for making sarcastic remarks to elderly shoppers, things like, *You sure you need these cookies, fat granny?* He has been told he will be fired the next time he is disrespectful, which is fine with him. He doesn't give a shit what any of them say. Dirt cakes the soles of his feet like calloused hooves as he stands on the asphalt in front of the bowling alley, smoking, guzzling, or ingesting whatever gifts his flock of disciples brings to him. He likes to make and hold eye contact until it makes people nervous.

When Agnes Hayes sees the boy bagging groceries in the market, her heart surges with pity. His complexion is blotched and infected, his hair long and oily. "Don't I know you?" she asks, but he doesn't even look up, his arms all inked with reptiles and knives and what looks like a religious symbol. Now she has spent the day trying to place him. She taught so many of them but their names and faces run together. In the three years since retirement, she has missed them more than she ever dreamed. Some days she even drives her car and parks near the high school to watch them, to somehow glimpse all that energy and to once again feel it in her own pulse. She still drives Edwin's copper-colored Electra, and has ever since he died almost two years ago. She would never have retired had she seen his death coming and with it an end to all their plans about where they wanted to go and what they wanted to do. One day she was complaining about plastic golf balls strewn all over the living room and the next she was calling 911 knowing even as she dialed and begged for someone to *please help* that it was too late.

The school is built on the same land where she herself went to school. She had once marched there, her clarinet held in her young hands while she stepped high with the marching band. Edwin's cigar is there in the ashtray, stinking as always, only now she loves the stink, can't get enough of it, wishes that she had never complained and made him go out to the garage or down to the basement to smoke. She wishes he were sitting there beside her, ringed in smoke. Their son, Preston, is clear across the country, barely in touch.

Sometimes creepy crawling involves only the car, cruising slowly through a driveway, headlights turned off, gravel crunching. There are lots of dogs. Lots of sensor lights. Lots of security systems, or at least the signs that *say* there is a system. The boy trusts nothing and no one. He believes in jiggling knobs and trying windows. When asked one time by a guidance counselor feigning compassion and concern what he did believe in, he said, "Not a goddamn thing." But, of course, he did. Anyone drawing breath has something he believes in, even if it is only that life sucks and there's no reason to live. Tonight he has announced that it is Lauren's turn to prove herself. She is a pretty girl behind the wall of heavy black eye makeup and black studded clothing. She wants out of the car but she owes him fifty dollars. He makes it sound like if she doesn't pay it back soon he'll take it out in sex. She is only here in the first place to get back at the boy she loved enough to do everything he asked. She wants him to worry about her, to want her, to think about that night at the campground the way that she does.

The leader reminds her often that he was there for her when no one else was. He listened to her story about the squeaky-clean asshole boyfriend, feeding her sips of cheap wine and stroking her dyed black hair the whole while she cried and talked and later reeled and heaved on all fours in a roadside ditch.

"He's an asswipe," the boy had said. "He used you." And then later when she woke just before dawn with her head pounding and her body filled with the sick knowledge that she had to go home and face her parents, he reminded her again how much she needed him, couldn't survive without him. "I didn't leave you," he said. "Could've easily fucked you and didn't."

And now she is here and the boy who broke her heart is out with someone else or maybe just eating dinner with his parents and talking about where he might choose to go to school. He is a boy who always smells clean, even right off the track, where he runs long distance, his thigh muscles like hard ropes, his lungs healthy and strong. He might be at the movies and she wishes she were there, too—the darkness, the popcorn. She wishes she were anywhere else. She had wanted her parents to restrict her after that night, to say she couldn't go anywhere for weeks and weeks, but they did something so much worse: they said how disappointed they were, that they had given up, how she would have to work really hard to regain their trust, and by *trust* it seems they meant *love*.

The leader is talking about how he hates their old math teacher. "And I know where she lives, too." He circles the block, drives slowly past a neat gray Colonial with a bright red door, the big Electra parked in the drive. "What's the magic word?" he mimics in a high southern voice and reaches over to grab Lauren's thigh then inches up, gripping harder as if daring her to move. He motions for her to unzip her jeans, wanting her to just sit there that way, silver chain from her navel grazing the thin strip of nylon that covers her. Lower, he says, even though there is another boy in the backseat hearing every word. She feels cold but doesn't say a word. Her shoes and jacket and purse are locked in the trunk of his car. "For safekeeping," he had said. She is about to readjust the V of denim when he swings the car off the side of the road behind a tall hedge of ligustrum, where they are partially hidden but can still see the house. "Like this," he says and tugs, a seam ripping, and then he slides across the seat toward her, his mouth hard on her own as he forces her hand to his own zipper. The boy in the backseat lights a cigarette and she focuses on that, the sound, the smell; she can hear the paper burn.

ERIN AND HER FRIEND, Tina, sit in the backseat, and Gregory is in the front with his Power Rangers sleeping bag rolled up at his feet. Paula will drop him off at the party and then go to the cinema and then she will still have time to sit and collect herself before driving seven miles down the interstate to the Days Inn where he will be waiting. The children have said that this car—their dad's—smells like old farts and jelly beans. They say he saves up all day at the bank and then rips all the way home. Gregory acts this out, and with each "ewww" and laugh from the girls, he gets a little more confident and louder. He says their grandmother smells like diarrhea dipped in peppermint and their grandfather is chocolate vomick. They are having a wonderful time mainly because it's daring, the way he is testing Paula, the way they all are waiting for her to intervene and reprimand, but she is so distracted she forgets to be a good mother. When he turns and scrutinizes her with a mischievous look, she snaps back.

"Not acceptable, young man, and you know it," she says, but really she is worried that they are right and that *she* will smell like old farts and jelly beans when she arrives at the motel. Her cell phone buzzes against her hip and she knows that he is calling to see if they are on schedule, calling to make sure that she doesn't stand him up again.

"Aren't you going to answer that?" Erin says. "Who is it, Dad looking for underwear? Some lame friend in need of a heart-to-heart?" The laughing continues as Paula turns on the street where a crowd of eight-year-olds and sleeping bags are gathered in the front yard of a small brick ranch.

"One of my lame friends, I'm sure," she answers, but with the words pictures him there in the room, maybe already undressed, a glass of wine poured. They have already said so much in their little notes that it feels like they have not only already made love but done so for so long that they are already needing to think of new things to do. Her pulse races and she slams on brakes when Gregory screams, "Stop!"

"Pay attention, Mom," Gregory says. "See, they're everywhere." She thinks he means her lame friends or kids at the party, but he picks up one of those little gourmet jelly beans, tosses it at his sister, and then jumps from the car. "Thanks, Mom," he says, and Paula waves to the already frazzled-looking mother who has taken this on. Thank you, Ronald Reagan. That's when the jelly bean frenzy started. And then after her husband said something cute and trite about sharing the desires of a president, since he was now a vice president at the bank, all his workers gave him jelly beans, because what else can you give to someone you don't know at all who has power and authority over you? He got all kinds of jelly beans. And now if people at the bank hear about the neighborhood wildlife, that will be the theme of the next many years of useless presents—coyote and raccoon and bat figurines and mugs and mugs and more mugs. She will write and send all those thank you notes. She will take it all to Goodwill.

SOMETIMES AGNES WATCHES television in the dark. She likes a lot of these new shows that are all about humiliating people until they confess that they are fat and need to lose weight or that they are inept workers who need to be fired or bad members of a team who need to be rejected and banished from the island. Her pug, Oliver, died not long after Edwin, and she misses the way he used to paw and tug and make a little nest at the foot of her bed. She misses the sounds of his little snorts in the night. How could there have been a moment in life when she wished for this? The quiet. The lack of activity and noise. The clock ticks, the refrigerator hums. She could call Preston. She could give him an apology whether she owes it or not. What she could say is that she is so sorry they misunderstood one another.

Or she could call him and pretend nothing had ever happened. She keeps thinking of the boy at the grocery, trying to place what year she taught him. Who were his parents? What is his name? There were some children she gave things to over the years, her own son's outgrown clothes and shoes, but then she stopped, dumping it all at the church instead because the children never acted the same afterwards and that bothered her. They never said thank you and they never looked her in the eye, as if she had never made a difference in their lives, and that was what hurt so much when she thought of Preston, how easily he had let a few things make him forget all that she had done for him in his life. She stated the truth is all. When Preston planned to marry Dee, Agnes told him how people might talk about them, might call their children names.

Right after Edwin's funeral, he called her Miss Christian Ethics, Miss Righteous Soul. He told her he wished he could stay and dig into all that ham and Jell-O but that Dee was at the Holiday Inn waiting for him. "They let dogs stay there, too," he said as he lingered over his father's prize rod and reel that she had handed to him. He put it back and left. She hasn't seen him since. Now her chest is heavy with the memory and her head and arm and side ache.

THE PARKING LOT STRETCHES for miles it seems, kids everywhere in packs, snuggly couples, the occasional middle-age settled-looking couple Paula envies more than all the others. The Cinema Fourteen Plex looms up ahead like Oz, like a big bright fake city offering any- and everything, a smorgasbord of action and emotion as varied as the jelly bean connoisseur basket her husband's secretary sent at Christmas, a woman Paula has so often wished would become something more. Wouldn't that be easier?

"He's here," Tina says and points to where a tall skinny kid in a letter jacket is pacing along the curb. "Oh my God. Oh my God."

"Puhleeze," Erin says, sounding way too old. "Chill out. He's *just* a *boy*." And then they collapse in another round of laughter and are out of the car and gone. Paula's hip is buzzing again. Buzzing and buzzing. What if it's Gregory and the sleepover is canceled? Or he fell on the skate ramp and broke something or needs stitches and her husband can't be found because he's out in the woods with a flashlight looking for wildlife? Or maybe her husband really does need her. He just got a call that his mother died. Does she know where he put the Havahart trap? And when is the last time she saw *their* cat?

Lauren is feeling frightened. The other boy, the one from the backseat, who is always quiet and refuses to talk about the bruises on his face and arms, has announced he's leaving. He can't do this anymore. The leader calls him a pussy. The leader says that if he leaves that's it, no more rides, no more pot, no more anything except he'll catch him some dark night and beat the shit out of him. "I'll beat you worse than whatever goes on in that trash house of yours," he says, but the boy keeps walking, and Lauren feels herself wanting to yell out for him to wait for her. She has always found him scary and disgusting but now she admires his ability to put one foot in front of the other. He says he's bored with it all—lame amateur shit—but she sees a fear in him as recognizable as her own. "Let him go," she whispers. She is watching the flicker of television light in the teacher's upstairs window. "Please. Can't we just ride around or something."

"Afraid you won't get any more tonight?" he asks and leans in so close she can smell his breath, oddly sweet with Dentyne. The lost possibility of his features makes her sad, eyes you might otherwise think a beautiful shade of blue, dimple in the left cheek. He pulls a coiled rope from under the seat. "You gonna stay put or do I need to tie you up?" She forces herself to laugh, to assure him that she will stay put, but she makes the mistake of glancing at the key in the ignition so he reaches and takes it.

She cautions herself to keep breathing, to act like she's with him. "Next one," she says. "I need to collect myself."

"Well, you just collect," he says. "I'll be back to deal with you in a minute." She doesn't ask what he plans to do. His outlines of all the ways such an event might go are lengthy and varied, some of them tame and pointless and others not pretty at all. He has already said he wants to scare the hell out of the old woman, let *her* know what it feels like to have someone make you say *please* and *thank you* every goddamn day. The girl watches him move into the darkness, numb fingers struggling to finally zip her pants back up, to pretend that his rough fingertips never touched her there. She will get out and run. She will leave the door open and crawl through the hedge until she reaches the main road. She will call her parents, beg for their forgiveness. There is no way now to get her shoes or phone but she moves and keeps moving. She thinks of her bed and how good it will feel to crawl between clean sheets, to stare at the faces of all the dolls collected before everything in her life seemed to go so bad. Now all the things she has been so upset about mean nothing. So what if she let the handsome clean-smelling track star do everything he wanted to do. She liked it, too, didn't she? Not making the soccer team last year. Being told on college day that she had no prayer of getting into any of the schools she had listed—most of them ones he was considering if he could run track. Losing or getting rejected. That happens to a lot of people, doesn't it? She can still find something she's good at, go *somewhere*. But now, she just wants to get home, to shower herself clean with the hottest water she can stand, to soap and scrub and wrap up in a flannel robe. She once watched her uncle skin a catfish, tearing the tight skin from the meat like an elastic suit, and she keeps thinking of the sound it made, a sound that made her want to pull her her jacket close, to hide and protect her own skin. She feels that way now, only there's nothing to pull around her, the night air much cooler than she'd thought—and she keeps thinking she hears him behind her so she moves faster. She is almost to the main road, the busy intersection, the rows of cars heading toward the cinema. Her foot is bleeding, a sliver of glass, and she is pinned at a corner, lines upon lines of cars waiting for the light to change.

PAULA'S CELL PHONE buzzes again and she takes a deep breath and answers. "Where are you?" he asks. She can hear the impatience, perhaps a twinge of anger, and his voice does not match the way she remembers him sounding there in the stairwell. When she pictures his face or reads his tiny penciled scrawl, it's a different voice, like it's been dubbed.

"Almost there," she says and tries to sound flirtatious, leaving him a promise of making up for lost time. Then she glances out her window and sees a girl in a torn shirt and barefooted she thinks she recognizes. They certainly won't let her in the theater that way. The girl is so familiar, and then Paula remembers, her daughter's school, story time in the library. But that was years ago when the girl's hair was light brown and pulled up in a high ponytail. She knows exactly who she is. This is a girl parents caution their *good* girls against. She is rumored to be bulimic. She locks herself in the school bathroom and cuts her arms. She once tried to overdose on vodka and aspirin and had to have her stomach pumped. She gives blowjobs in the stairwell of the high school in exchange for drugs. She has blackened ghoulish eyes and jet-black hair, silver safety pins through her eyebrows and lip. Paula has heard parents whispering about her at various school functions. They say, "Last year she was perfectly normal, and now this. She was a B student with some artistic talent and a somewhat pretty face, and now this." She is the "Don't" poster child of this town, the local object lesson in how quickly a child can go bad.

AGNES IS TRYING to remember what exactly it was she said to anger Preston so. She had tried to make it complimentary, something about skin like café au lait. She had often seen black people described that way in stories, coffee and chocolates, conjuring delicious smells instead of those like the bus station or fish market across the river, which is what a lot of people might associate with black people. Her maid once used a pomade so powerful smelling that Agnes had to ask that she please stop wearing it, but certainly Agnes never held that against the woman; she couldn't help being born into a culture that thought that was the thing to do.

"Sometimes it's not even *what* stupid thing you say," Preston shouted, the vein in his forehead buckling like it might burst. "It's *how* you say it. So, so, goddamned godlike." He spit the word and shook all over, hands clenched into fists. But now she wants him to come back and be with her. She didn't know coffee would be insulting. She is going through her phone numbers, she has it somewhere. That same day she reminded him that even the president of the United States said things like that. The president had once referred to his grandchildren as "the little brown ones." Why is that okay and chocolate and coffee are not?

It's your mom, she practices now. *Please talk to me, Preston*. She is dialing when she hears something down on her front porch. The wind? Her cat? There was a flyer in her mailbox just this evening saying how she should not leave the cat outside.

LAUREN SHIVERS AS SHE stands there on the corner. She expects to hear his car roar up near her any second from now and wonders what she will possibly do when that happens. She will have to tell her parents that she lost her purse, it got stolen, and her shoes and her jacket. She shudders with the thought of the boy pawing through her personal things, a picture of the track star cut from the school newspaper, a poem she was writing about the ocean, a pale pink rabbit's foot she has carried since sixth grade when she won the school math bee with it in her pocket. The light is about to change and she concentrates on that instead of imagining her parents' reaction. Just once she wishes one of them would pull her close and say, *Please, tell me what's wrong*, and then she would. She would start talking and not stop, like a dam breaking through; she would tell them so many things if there were really such a thing as unconditional love. But instead they will say, *What is wrong with you? Why are you doing this to us? Do you know what people are saying about you?*

"Do you need a ride?" A woman in an old black Audi leans out the window and motions her to hurry. "I know you from school."

She does know the woman, the mother of a girl in her class, a girl who makes good grades and doesn't get in trouble. Not a popular girl, just a normal girl. A nice girl who smiles shyly and will let you copy her notes if you get behind. Erin from Algebra I freshman year. This is Erin's mother.

She hears a car slowing in the lane beside her and runs to get in with the woman just as the light changes. "Thank you."

"My daughter goes to your school," the woman says. She is wearing a low-cut camisole with a pretty silver necklace. Her black sweater is soft and loose around her shoulders. The car smells like crayons and the woman's cologne. "I'm sorry my car is so messy. My husband's car, that is." Her cell phone buzzes in the cup holder but she ignores it. "Where are you going, sweetheart?" she asks. "It's too chilly to be out without shoes and long sleeves." Something in her voice brings tears to the girl's eyes, and then her crying is uncontrollable. The woman just keeps driving, circling first the cinema and then many of the neighborhoods around the area. The girl sinks low in her seat when they pass the teacher's house, that old Pontiac still parked behind the hedge. She can't allow herself to imagine what he is doing, what he will do when he finds her gone. They drive out to the interstate and make a big loop, the woman patting her shoulder from time to time, telling her it's okay, that nothing can be that bad. Every third or fourth time she asks for the girl's address, but for now she just wants to be here in this car riding. The woman's cell phone keeps buzzing and buzzing. Once she answers it to the loud voice of her daughter from the movie lobby saying she will need a ride home after all. "Are you mad, Mom?" the girl screams. "Is that okay?" And the woman assures that it is okay. It is fine. She will be there. Then she answers her phone and says she saw their cat early this morning. And then, apologizing when it rings again, she answers and says little at all, except that so much has happened, she just might not get there at all. "In fact," she whispers, "I know I can't get there." And Lauren knows there is a good chance that she is part of what has happened, but the heat is blowing on her cold feet and the woman has the radio turned down low with classical music and her eyelids are so heavy she can barely keep them open. When she was little and couldn't sleep, her parents would sometimes put her in a warm car to ride her around. Her dad called it a "get lost" drive and he let her make all the choices, turn here, turn there, turn there again, and then she would relax while he untangled the route and led them back home, by which time she would be near or already asleep. There was never any doubt that he could find the way home and that she would wake to find herself already tucked in her bed or in his arms being taken there.

Preston's answering machine comes on and Agnes is about to speak but then she hears the noise again and puts down the phone. She wishes she would find Preston there—Preston and Dee—waiting to embrace her and start all over again. Preston in his letter jacket like all those nights she waited up for him and said, "Where have you been, young man?" And Edwin would be in the basement smoking and Oliver would be rooting around at the foot of her bed.

Her chest is tight with the worry of it all. She swallows and opens the door.

Nothing.

"Here kitty," she calls in a faint voice. She steps out on the stoop into the chilly air. The sky is clear overhead, a sliver of a moon. There is a car parked way down at the end of her drive, just the front bumper showing beyond the hedge. It wasn't there when she came home. Perhaps someone had a flat or ran out of gas. She calls the cat again and hears leaves crunching around the side of the house. She waits, expecting to see it slink around the corner, but then nothing. But there is more noise beyond the darkness where she can't see. And it is coming closer, short quick sounds, footsteps in the leaves. She is backing into the house when she thinks she sees something much larger than the cat slip around the corner near her kitchen door. She pulls her sweater close and pushes the door to, turns the dead bolt.

The flyer talked about coyotes and how they have been spotted all over town.

THE GIRL FINALLY tells Paula where she lives, a neighborhood out from town and in the other direction of the motel. Paula's cell phone beeps with yet another message but now she ignores it. She doesn't want to hear what he has to say now that he has had time to shape an answer to her standing him up yet again. She parks in front of a small stucco house. The front porch is lit with a yellow bulb; all the drapes are pulled closed.

"I'm happy to walk you up," Paula says, but the girl shakes her head. She says thank you without making eye contact and then gets out, moves across the yard in slow careful steps. Paula waits to see if a parent comes out, but the girl slips in and recloses the door and everything is still.

Paula sits there in the dark as if expecting something to happen. And then she slips off the cardigan and pulls her turtleneck over her head. The message is waiting. He might be saying this is the last time he will do this, he has wasted too much time on her already. *Why are you fucking with me?* he might ask. Or *Who do you think you are?* The chances of him saying how he understands completely and they will try again some other better time are slim. She imagines him there in the room, bare chested and waiting, already thinking about his other options, his better options. And she imagines her own house and her return: sink full of dirty dishes, Power Ranger figures everywhere, a litter box that needs scooping and clothes that need washing and an empty pantry that would have been filled had she not been out buying lingerie all day.

She saw a coyote just last week but she didn't report it. She was standing at the kitchen window and glanced out to see a tall skinny shepherd mix, only just as her mind was shaping the thought about someone letting his dog run loose in the neighborhood, it came to her that this was *not* a dog. It was wild and fearful looking, thin and hungry, and she felt a kinship as they stood frozen and staring at one another. Everyone wants something.

THE LEADER CAN SEE her in there, old bat, holding her chest and shaking. She looks like a puppet, the jerks of her old bitch of a body in time with his jiggling the knob. *I wore your fucking boy's shirt,* he will say. *Thank you so much. That little Polo fucker really helped turn my life around.* She lifts the phone and pulls the cord around the corner where he can't see her so he jiggles harder, leans the weight of his body against the door. *Loafers! Neckties! F in fucking math.* He creeps around and climbs high enough on a trellis to see that she is slumped down in a chair with the receiver clutched against her chest. "Say the magic word," he says and covers his fist with his shirt before punching out the window. "Say it."

When Paula pulls up to the theater, Erin and Tina are waiting. A tall thin boy in a letter jacket trails alongside Tina, his hand in her hip pocket in a familiar way, and then they kiss before the girls get in the car. Paula is about to mention the girl she picked up but then thinks better of it. She wants to say things like *don't you ever* but then the sound of her daughter's laughter makes her stop.

"I can't believe you, like, ate face in front of my mom," Erin says, and Tina blushes and grins. She is a girl with cleavage and braces, betwixt and between.

"Jesus, Mom, let some air in this stinkhole car." Erin laughs and then the two girls talk over the movie and everyone they saw there as if Paula is not even present. She can't stop thinking about the girl and how she came to be on that busy corner with no shoes, how she looks so different from that clean-faced little girl in a library chair, and yet she is one and the same. And what will she write and slip to her coworker on Monday, or will she avoid him altogether and pretend nothing ever happened, that she never ventured from her own darkened den in search of excitement? She imagines the coyotes living as her husband has described, little nests under piles of brush, helpless cubs curled there and waiting for the return of their mother.

"I'm sorry if I messed up your time with your lame friend," Erin says sarcastically and then leans in close. "Really, Momsy, I am." She air kisses Paula and smiles a sincere thanks before turning back to her friend with a shriek of something she can't believe she forgot to tell, something about cheating, someone getting caught with a teacher's grade book. She has licorice twists braided and tied around her throat like a necklace and her breath is sweet with Milk Duds.

THE OLD WOMAN is dead or acting dead, the recorded voice from the receiver on her chest telling her to please hang up and try her call again. It's one of those houses where everything is in place, little useless bullshit glass things nobody wants. She looks as miserable dead as she did alive. It makes him want to trash the place, but why bother now? He didn't kill her. He didn't do a thing but pop out a pane of glass. He searches around and then, carefully, using his shirt so as not to leave a print, takes a golf ball from the basket beside the fireplace and places it down in the broken glass. Television is too big to lift, no purse in sight, not even a liquor cabinet. She gives him the creeps and so do all the people looking out from portraits and photographs. He'll tell the girl that he just scared the old bitch, threatened to tie her up and put a bullet in her head until she cried and begged his mercy and forgiveness. He'll say he left her alive and grateful.

THE MOON IS HIGH in the bright clear sky when Paula ventures outside to look for their cat. She pulls her sweater close and steps away from the light of the house, the woods around her spreading into darkness. Her husband is sleeping and Erin is on the phone. There were no messages other than the one on her cell phone, still trapped there and waiting. She hears a distant siren, the wind in the trees, the bass beat from a passing car. *Please*, she thinks. *Please.* She is about to go inside for a flashlight when she hears the familiar bell and then sees the cat slinking up from the dark woods, her manner cool and unaffected.

INTERVENTION

THE INTERVENTION IS NOT Marilyn's idea but it might as well be. She is the one who has talked too much. And she has agreed to go along with it, nodding and murmuring an "all right" into the receiver while Sid dozes in front of the evening news. They love watching the news. Things are so horrible all over the world that it makes them feel lucky just to be alive. Sid is sixty-five. He is retired. He is disappearing before her very eyes.

"Okay, Mom?" She jumps with her daughter's voice, which is loud to be heard over the noise at her end of the phone—a house full of children, a television blasting, whines about homework—all those noises you complain about for years only to wake one day and realize you would sell your soul to go back for another chance to do it right.

"Yes, yes," she says.

"Is he drinking right now?"

MARILYN HAS NEVER heard the term *intervention* before her daughter, Sally, introduces it and showers her with a pile of literature. Sally's husband has a master's in social work and considers himself an expert on this topic as well as many others. Most of Sally's sentences begin with "Rusty says," to the point that Sid long ago made up a little spoof about "Rusty says," turning it into a game like Simon says. "Rusty says put your hands on your head," Sid said the first time, once the newly married couple were out of earshot. "Rusty says put your head up your ass." Marilyn howled with laughter just as she always has. Sid can always make her laugh. Usually she laughs longer and harder. A stranger would have assumed that she was the one slinging back the vodka. Twenty years earlier, the stranger would have been right.

SALLY AND RUSTY have now been married for a dozen years—three kids and two Volvos and several major vacations (that were so educational they couldn't have been any fun) behind them—and still, Marilyn and Sid cannot look each other in the eye while Rusty is talking without breaking into giggles like a couple of junior high school students. And Marilyn knows junior high behavior; she taught language arts for many years. She is not shocked when a boy wears the crotch of his pants down around his knees and she knows that Sean Combs has gone from that perfectly normal name to Sean "Puffy" Combs to Puff Daddy to P. Diddy. She knows that the kids make a big circle at dances so that the ones in the center can do their grinding without getting in trouble and she has learned that there are many perfectly good words that you cannot use in front of humans who are being powered by hormonal surges. She once asked her class, "How will you ever get ahead?" only to have them all—even the most pristine honor roll girls—collapse in hysterics. Just last year—her final one—she had learned never to ask if they had hooked up with so and so, learning quickly that this no longer meant "locating a person" but "having sex." She could not hear the term now without laughing. She told Sid it reminded her of the time two dogs got stuck in the act just outside her classroom window. The children were out of control, especially when the assistant principal stepped out there armed with a garden hose, which didn't faze the lust-crazed dogs in the slightest. When the female—a scrawny shepherd mix—finally took off running, the male—who was quite a bit smaller—was stuck and forced to hop along behind her like a jackrabbit. "His thang is stuck," one of the girls yelled and broke out in a dance, prompting others to do the same.

"Sounds like me," Sid said that night when they were lying there in the dark. "I'll follow you anywhere."

Now, as Sid dozes, she goes and pulls out the envelope of information about family intervention. She never should have told Sally that she had concerns, never should have mentioned that there were times when she watched Sid pull out of the driveway only to catch herself imagining that this could be the last time she ever saw him.

"Why do you think that?" Sally asked, suddenly attentive and leaning forward in her chair. Up until that minute, Marilyn had felt invisible while Sally rattled on and on about drapes and chairs and her book group and Rusty's accolades. "Was he visibly drunk? Why do you let him drive when he's that way?"

"He's never visibly drunk," Marilyn said then, knowing that she had made a terrible mistake. They were at the mall, one of those forced outings that Sally had read was important. Probably an article Rusty read first called something like: "Spend Time with Your Parents So You Won't Feel Guilty When You Slap Them in a Urine-Smelling Old Folks' Home." Rusty's parents are already in such a place; they share a room and eat three meals on room trays while they watch television all day. Rusty says they're ecstatic. They have so much to tell that they are living for the next time Rusty and Sally and the kids come to visit.

"I pray to God I never have to rely on such," Sid said when

she relayed this bit of conversation. She didn't tell him the other parts of the conversation at the mall, how even when she tried to turn the topic to shoes and how it seemed to her that either shoes had gotten smaller or girls had gotten bigger (nine was the average size for most of her willowy eighth-grade girls), Sally bit into the subject like a pit bull.

"How much does he drink in a day?" Sally asked. "You must know. I mean *you* are the one who takes out the garbage and does the shopping."

"He helps me."

"A fifth?"

"Sid loves to go to the Harris Teeter. They have a book section and everything."

"Rusty has seen this coming for years." Sally leaned forward and gripped Marilyn's arm. Sally's hands were perfectly manicured with pale pink nails and a great big diamond. "He asked me if Dad had a problem before we ever got married." She gripped tighter. "Do you know that? That's a dozen years."

"I wonder if the Oriental folks have caused this change in the shoe sizes?" Marilyn pulled away and glanced over at Lady Foot Locker as if to make a point. She knows that "Oriental" is not the thing to say. She knows to say "Asian," and though Sally thinks that she and Rusty are the ones who teach her all of these things, the truth is that she learned it all from her students. She knew to say Hispanic and then Latino, probably before Rusty did, because she sometimes watches the MTV channel so that she's up on what is happening in the world and thus in the lives of children at the junior high. Shocking things, yes, but also important. Sid has always believed that it is better to be educated even if what is true makes you uncomfortable or depressed. Truth is, she can understand why some of these youngsters want to say motherfucker this and that all the time. Where *are* their mommas after all; and where are their daddies? Rusty needs to watch MTV. He needs to watch that and *Survivor* and all the other reality shows. He's got children, and unless he completely rubs off on them, they will be normal enough to want to know what's happening out there in the world.

"Asian," Sally whispered. "You really need to just throw out that word *Oriental* unless you're talking about lamps and carpets. I know what you're doing, too."

"What about *queer*? I hear that word is okay again."

"You have to deal with Dad's problem," Sally said.

"I hear that even the homosapiens use that word, but it might be the kind of thing that only one who is a member can use, kind of like—"

"Will you stop it?" Sally interrupted and banged her hand on the table.

"Like the *n* word," Marilyn said. "The black children in my class used it but it would have been terrible for somebody else to."

Sally didn't even enunciate "African American" the way she

usually does. "This doesn't work anymore!" Sally's face reddened, her voice a harsh whisper. "So cut the Gracie Allen routine."

"I loved Gracie, so did Sid. What a woman." Marilyn rummaged her purse for a tissue or a stick of gum, anything so as not to have to look at Sally. Sally looks so much like Sid they could be in a genetics textbook: those pouty lips and hard blue eyes, prominent cheekbones and dark curly hair. Sid always told people his mother was a Cherokee and his father a Jew, which made him a Cherojew, which Marilyn said sounded like TheraFlu, which they both like even when they don't have colds, so he went with Jewokee instead. Marilyn's ancestors were all Irish so she and Sid called their children the Jewokirish. Sid said that the only thing that could save the world would be when everybody was so mixed up with this blood and that that nobody could pronounce the resulting tribe name. It would have to be a symbol like the name of the Artist Formerly Known as Prince, which was something she had just learned and had to explain to Sid. She doubts that Sally and Rusty even know who Prince is, or Nelly for that matter. Nelly is the reason all the kids are wearing Band-Aids on their faces, which is great for those just learning to shave.

"Remember that whole routine Dad and I made up about ancestry?" Marilyn asked. She was able to look up now, Sally's hands squeezing her own, Rusty's hands on her shoulders. If she had had an ounce of energy left in her body, she would have run into Lord and Taylor and gotten lost in the mirrored cosmetic section.

"The fact that you brought all this up is a cry for help whether you admit it or not," Sally said. "And we are here, Mother. We are here for you."

She wanted to ask why "Mother"—what happened to Mom and Mama and Mommy—but she couldn't say a word.

There are some nights when Sid is dozing there that she feels frightened. She puts her hand on his chest to feel his heart. She puts her cheek close to his mouth to feel the breath. She did the same to Sally and Tom when they were children, especially with Tom, who came first. She was up and down all night long in those first weeks making sure that he was breathing, still amazed that this perfect little creature belonged to them. Sometimes Sid would wake and do it for her, even though his work as a grocery distributor in those days caused him to get up at five a.m. The times he went to check, he would return to their tiny bedroom and lunge toward her with a perfect Dr. Frankenstein imitation: "He's alive!" followed by maniacal laughter. In those days she joined him for a drink just as the sun was setting. It was their favorite time of day and they both always resisted the need to flip on a light and return to life. The ritual continued for years and does to this day. When the children were older they would make jokes about their parents, who were always "in the dark," and yet those pauses, the punctuation marks of a marriage, could tell their whole history spoken and unspoken.

• • •

THE LITERATURE SAYS that an intervention is the most loving and powerful thing a loved one can do. That some family members might be apprehensive. Tom was apprehensive at first but he always has been; Tom is the noncombative child. He's an orthopedist living in Denver. Skiing is great for his health and his business. And his love life. He met the new wife when she fractured her ankle. Her marriage was already fractured, his broken, much to the disappointment of Marilyn and Sid, who found the first wife to be the most loving and open-minded of the whole bunch. The new wife, Sid says, is too young to have any opinions you give a damn about. In private they call her Snow Bunny.

Tom was apprehensive until the night he called after the hour she had told everyone was acceptable. "Don't call after nine unless it's an emergency," she had told them. "We like to watch our shows without interruption." But that night, while Sid dozed and the made-for-TV movie she had looked forward to ended up (as her students would say) sucking, she went to run a deep hot bath, and that's where she was, incapable of getting to the phone fast enough.

"Let the machine get it, honey," she called as she dashed with just a towel wrapped around her dripping body, but she wasn't fast enough. She could hear the slur in Sid's speech. He could not say *slalom* to save his soul, and instead of letting the moment pass, he kept trying and trying, "What the shit is wrong with my tongue, Tom? Did I have a goddamn stroke? Sllllmmmm—sla, sla—"

Marilyn ran and picked up the extension. "Honey, Daddy has taken some decongestants, bless his heart, full of a terrible cold. Go on back to sleep now, Sid, I've got it."

"I haven't got a goddamned cold. Your mother's a kook!" He laughed and waved to where she stood in the kitchen, a puddle of suds and water at her feet. "She's a good-looking naked kook. I see her bony ass right now."

"Hang up, Tommy," she said. "I'll call you right back from the other phone. Daddy is right in the middle of his program."

"Yeah right," Tom said.

By the time she got Sid settled down, dried herself off and put on her robe, Tom's line was busy, and she knew before even dialing Sally that hers would be busy, too. It was a full hour later, Sid fast asleep in the bed they had owned for thirty-five years, when she finally got through, and then it was to a more serious Tom than she had heard in years. Not since he left the first wife and signed off on the lives of her grandchildren in a way that prevented her from seeing them more than once a year if she was lucky. She could get mad at him for *that.* So could Sid.

"We're not talking about my life right now," he said. "I've given Dad the benefit of the doubt for years, but Sally and Rusty are right."

"Rusty! You're the one who said he was full of it," she screamed. "And now you're on his side?"

"I'm on your side, Mom, your side."

She let her end fall silent and concentrated on Sid's breath. He's alive.

SID LIKES TO DRIVE and Marilyn has always felt secure with him there behind the wheel. Every family vacation, every weekend gathering. He was always voted the best driver of the bunch, even when a whole group had gathered down at the beach for a summer cookout, where both men and women drank too much. Sid mostly drank beer in those days; he kept an old Pepsi-Cola cooler he once won throwing baseballs at tin cans at the county fair iced down with Falstaff and Schlitz. They still have that cooler. It's out in the garage on the top shelf, long ago replaced with little red-and-white Playmates. Tom gave Sid his first Playmate, which has remained a family joke until this day. And Marilyn drank then. She liked the taste of beer but not the bloat. She loved to water-ski and they took turns behind a friend's powerboat. The men made jokes when the women dove in to cool off. They claimed that warm spots emerged wherever the women had been and that if they couldn't hold their beer any better than that, they should switch to girl drinks. And so they did. A little wine or a mai tai, vodka martinis. Sid had a book that told him how to make everything, and Marilyn enjoyed buying little colored toothpicks and umbrellas to dress things up when it was their turn to host. She loved rubbing her body with baby oil and iodine and letting the warmth of the sun and salty air soak in while the radio played and the other women talked. They all smoked cigarettes then. They all had little leather cases with fancy lighters tucked inside.

Whenever Marilyn sees the Pepsi cooler she is reminded of those days. Just married. No worries about skin cancer or lung cancer. No one had varicose veins. No one talked about cholesterol. None of their friends were addicted to anything other than the sun and the desire to get up on one ski—to slalom. The summer she was pregnant with Tom—compliments of a few too many mai tais, Sid told the group—she sat on the dock and sipped her ginger ale. The motion of the boat made her queasy, as did anything that had to do with poultry. "It ain't the size of the ship but the motion of the ocean," Sid was fond of saying in those days, and she laughed every time. Every time he said it, she complimented his liner and the power of his steam. They batted words like *throttle* and *wake* back and forth like a birdie until finally, at the end of the afternoon, she'd go over and whisper, "Ready to dock?"

Her love for Sid then was overwhelming. His hair was thick and he tanned a deep smooth olive without any coaxing. He was everything she had ever wanted, and she told him this those summer days as they sat through the twilight time. She didn't tell him how sometimes she craved the vodka tonics she had missed. Even though many of her friends continued drinking and smoking through their pregnancies, she would allow herself only one glass of wine with dinner. When she bragged about this during

Sally's first pregnancy, she expected to be congratulated for her modest intake, but Sally was horrified. "My God, Mother," she said. "Tom is lucky there's not something bad wrong with him!"

Tom set the date for the intervention. As hard as it was for Rusty to relinquish his power even for a minute as leader of the posse, it made perfect sense given that Tom had to take time off from his practice and fly all the way from Denver. The snow bunny was coming, too, even though she really didn't know Sid at all. Sometimes over the past five years, Marilyn had called up the first wife just to hear her voice, or even better the voice of one or more of her grandchildren on the answering machine. Now there was a man's name included in the list of who wasn't home. She and Sid would hold the receiver between them, both with watering eyes, when they heard the voices they barely recognized. They didn't know about *69 until a few months ago when Margot, the oldest child, named for Sid's mother, called back. "Who is this?" she asked. She was growing up in Minnesota and now had an accent that Marilyn only knew from Betty White's character on *The Golden Girls*.

"Your grandmother, honey. Grandma Marilyn in South Carolina."

There was a long silence, and then the child began to speak rapidly, filling them in on all that was going on in her life. "Mom says you used to teach junior high," Margot said, and she and

Sid both grinned, somehow having always trusted that their daughter-in-law would not have turned on them as Tom had led them to believe.

Then Susan got on the phone, and as soon as she did, Marilyn burst into tears. "Oh Susie, forgive me," she said. "You know how much we love you and the kids."

"I know," she said. "And if Tom doesn't bring the kids to you, I will. I promise." Marilyn and Sid still believe her. They fantasize during the twilight hour that she will drive up one day and there they'll all be. Then, lo and behold, here will come Tom. "He'll see what a goddamned fool he's been," Sid says. "They'll hug and kiss and send Snow Bunny packing."

"And we'll all live happily ever after," Marilyn says.

"You can take that to the bank, baby," he says, and she hugs him close, whispers that he has to eat dinner before they can go anywhere.

"You know I'm a very good driver," she says, and he just shakes his head back and forth; he can list every ticket and fender bender she has had in her life.

THE INTERVENTION DAY is next week. Tom and Bunny plan to stay with Sally and Rusty an hour away so that Sid won't get suspicious. Already it is unbearable to her—this secret. There has only been one time in their whole marriage when she had a secret, and it was a disaster.

"What's wrong with you?" Sid keeps asking. "So quiet." His eyes have that somber look she catches once in awhile; it's a look of hurt, a look of disillusionment. It is the look that nearly killed them thirty-odd years ago.

THERE HAVE BEEN many phone calls late at night. Rusty knows how to set up conference calls and there they all are, Tom and Sally and Rusty talking nonstop. If he resists, we do this. If he gets angry, we do that. All the while, Sid dozes. Sometimes the car is parked crooked in the drive, a way that he never would have parked even two years ago, and she goes out in her housecoat and bedroom slippers to straighten it up so the neighbors won't think anything is wrong. She has repositioned the mailbox many times, touched up paint on the car and the garage that Sid didn't even notice. Sometimes he is too tired to move or undress, and she spreads a blanket over him in the chair. Recently she found a stash of empty bottles in the bottom of his golf bag. Empty bottles in the Pepsi cooler, the trunk of his car.

"I suspect he lies to you about how much he has," Rusty says. "We are taught not to ask an alcoholic how much he drinks but to phrase it in a way that accepts a lot of intake, such as 'How many fifths do you go through in a weekend?' "

"Sid doesn't lie to me."

"This is as much for you," Rusty says, and she can hear the impatience in his voice. "You are what we call an enabler."

She doesn't respond. She reaches and takes Sid's warm limp hand in her own.

"If you really love him," he pauses, gathering volume and force in his words, "you have to go through with this."

"It was really your idea, Mom," Sally says. "We all suspected as much but you're the one who really blew the whistle." Marilyn remains quiet, picturing herself like some kind of Nazi woman blowing a shrill whistle, dogs barking, flesh tearing. She can't answer; her head is swimming. "Admit it. He almost killed you when he went off the road. It's your side that would have smashed into the pole. You were lucky."

"I was driving," she says now, whispering so as not to wake him. "I almost killed him!"

"Nobody believed you, Marilyn," Rusty says, and she is reminded of the one and only student she has hated in her career, a smart-assed boy who spoke to her as if he were the adult and she were the child. Even though she knew better, knew that he was a little jerk, it had still bothered her.

"You're lucky Mr. Randolph was the officer on duty, Mom," Tom says. "He's not going to look the other way next time. He told me as much."

"And what about how you told me you have to hide his keys sometimes?" Sally asks. "What about that?"

"Where are the children?" Marilyn asks. "Are they hearing all of this?"

"No," Rusty says. "We won't tell this sort of thing until they're older and can learn from it."

"We didn't," she whispers and then ignores their questions. Didn't what? Didn't what?

"The literature says that there should be a professional involved," she says, and for a brief anxious moment, relishes their silence.

"Rusty is a professional," Sally says. "This is what he does for a living."

Sid lives for a living, she wanted to say, but she let it all go. They were coming, come hell or high water. She can't stop what she has put into motion, a rush of betrayal and shame pushing her back to a dark place she has not seen in years. Sid stirs and brings her hand up to his cheek.

SID NEVER TOLD the children anything. He never brought up anything once it had passed, unlike Marilyn, who sometimes gets stuck in a groove, spinning and spinning, deeper and deeper. Whenever anything in life—the approach of spring, the smell of gin, pine sap thawing and coming back to life—prompts her terrible memory, she cringes and feels the urge to crawl into a dark hole. She doesn't recognize that woman. That woman was sick. A sick foolish woman, a woman who had no idea that the best of life was in her hand. It was late spring and they went with a group to the lake. They hired babysitters round the clock, so the men could fish and the women could sun and shop and nobody had to be concerned for all the needs of the youngsters. The days began with coffee and Bloody Marys and ended with sloppy kisses on the sleeping brows of their babies. Sid was worried then. He was bucking for promotions right and left, taking extra shifts. He wanted to run the whole delivery service in their part of the state and knew that he could do it if he ever got the chance to prove himself. Then he would have normal hours, good benefits.

Marilyn had never even noticed Paula Edwards's husband before that week. She spoke to him, yes; she thought it was Paula's good fortune to have married someone who had been so successful so young. ("Easy when it's a family business and handed to you," Sid said, the only negative thing she ever heard him say about the man.) But there he was, not terribly attractive but very attentive. Paula was pregnant with twins and forced to a lot of bed rest. Even now, the words of the situation playing through Marilyn's mind shock her.

"You needed attention," Sid said when it all exploded in her face. "I'm sorry I wasn't there."

"Who are you, Jesus Christ?" she screamed. "Don't you hate me? Paula hates me!"

"I'm not Paula. And I'm not Jesus." He went to the cabinet and mixed a big bourbon and water. He had never had a drink that early in the day. "I'm a man who is very upset."

"At me!"

"At both of us."

She wanted him to hate her right then. She wanted him to make her suffer, make her pay. She had wanted him even at the time it was Paula's husband meeting her in the weeks following in dark, out-of-the-way parking lots—rest areas out on the interstate, rundown motels no one with any self-esteem would venture into. And yet there she had been. She bought the new underwear the way women so often do, as if that thin bit of silk could prolong the masquerade. Then later, afterwards, she had burned all the new garments in a huge puddle of gasoline, a flame so high the fire department came, only to find her stretched out on the grass of her front yard, sobbing. Her children, ages four and two, were there beside her, wide-eyed and frightened. "Mommy? Are you sick?" She felt those tiny hands pulling and pulling. "Mommy? Are you sad?" Paula's husband wanted sex. She could have been anyone those times he twisted his hands in her thick long hair, grown the way Sid liked it, and pulled her head down. He wanted her to scream out and tear at him. He liked it that way. Paula wasn't that kind of girl, but he knew that Marilyn was.

"But you're not," Sid told her in the many years to follow, the times when self-loathing overtook her body and reduced her to an anguished heap on the floor. "You're not that kind."

• • •

People knew. They had to know. But out of respect for Sid, they never said a word. Paula had twin girls and they moved to California, and to this day, they send a Christmas card with a brag letter much like the one that Sally and Rusty have begun sending. Something like: *We are brilliant and we are rich. Our lives are perfect. Don't you wish yours was as good?* If Sid gets the mail, he tears it up and never says a word. He did the same with the letter that Paula wrote to him when she figured out what was going on. Marilyn never saw what the letter said. She only heard Sid sobbing from the other side of a closed door, the children vigilant as they waited for him to come out. When his days of silence ended and she tried to talk, he simply put a finger up to her lips, his eyes dark and shadowed in a way that frightened her. He mixed himself a drink and offered her one as they sat and listened with relief to the giggles of the children playing outside. Sid had bought a sandbox and put it over the burned spot right there in the front yard. He said that in the fall when it was cooler he'd cover it with sod. He gave up on advancing to the top and settled instead on a budget and all the investments he could do to ensure college educations and decent retirement.

Her feelings each and every year when spring came had nothing to do with any lingering feelings she might have had about the affair—she had none. Rather her feelings were about the disgust she felt for herself—and the more disgusted she felt the more she needed some form of self-medication. For her, alcohol was the symptom of the greater problem, and she shuddered with recall of all the nights Sid had to scoop her up from the floor and carry her to bed. The times she left pots burning on the stove, the time Tom as a five-year-old sopped towels where she lay sick on the bathroom floor. "Mommy is sick," he told Sid, who stripped and bathed her, put cool sheets around her body, cool cloth to her head. It was the vision of her children standing there and staring at her, their eyes as somber and vacuous as Sid's had been that day he got Paula's letter, that woke her up.

"I'm through," she said. "I need help."

Sid backed her just as he always had. Rusty would have called him her enabler. He nursed her and loved her. He forgave her and forgave her. "I'm a bad chemistry experiment," she told Sid. Without him, she would not have survived.

ON THE DAY of the intervention, the kids come in meaning business, but then can't help but lapse into discussion about their own families and how great they all are. Snow Bunny wants a baby, which makes Sid laugh, even though Marilyn can tell he suspects something is amiss. Rusty has been promoted. He is thinking about going back to school to get his degree in psychology. They gather in the living room, Sid in his chair, a coffee cup on the table beside him. She knows there is bourbon in his cup but would never say a word. She doesn't have to. Sally sweeps by, grabs the cup, and then is in the kitchen sniffing its content.

Rusty gives the nod of a man in charge. Sid is staring at her, all the questions easily read: *Why are they here? Did you know they were coming? Why did you keep this from me?* She has to look away. She never should have let this happen. She should have found a way to bring Sid around to his own decision the way he had led her.

Now she wants to scream at the children that she did this to Sid. She wants to pull out the picture box and say: *This is me back when I was fucking my friend's husband while you were asleep in your beds. And this is me when I drank myself sick so that I could forget what a horrible woman and wife and mother I was. Here is where I passed out on the floor with a pan of hot grease on the stove and here is where I became so hysterical in the front yard that I almost burned the house down. I ruined the lawn your father worked so hard to grow. I ruined your father. I did this, and he never told you about how horrible I was. He protected me. He saved me.*

"WELL, SID," RUSTY BEGINS. "We have come together to be with you because we're concerned about you."

"We love you, Daddy, and we're worried."

"Mom is worried," Tom says, and as Sid turns to her, Marilyn has to look down. "Your drinking has become a problem, and we've come to get help for you."

I'm the drunk, she wants to say. *I was here first.*

"You're worried, honey?" Sid asks. "Why haven't you told me?"

SHE LOOKS UP NOW, first at Sid and then at Sally and Tom. If you live long enough, your children learn to love you from afar, their lives are front and center and elsewhere. Your life is only what they can conjure from bits and pieces. They don't know how it all fits together. They don't know all the sacrifices that have been made.

"We're here as what is called an intervention," Rusty says.

"Marilyn?" He is gripping the arms of his chair. "You knew this?"

"No," she says. "No, I didn't. I have nothing to do with this."

"Marilyn," Rusty rises from his chair, Sally right beside him. It's like the room has split in two and she is given a clear choice—the choice she wishes she had made years ago and then maybe none of this would have ever happened.

"We can take care of this on our own," she says. "We've taken care of far worse."

"Such as?" Tom asks. She has always wanted to ask him what he remembers from those horrible days. Does he remember finding her there on the floor? Does he remember her wishing to be dead?

"Water under the bridge," Sid says. "Water under the bridge." Sid stands, shoulders thrown back. He is still the tallest man in the room. He is the most powerful man. "You kids are great," he says. "You're great and you're right." He goes into the kitchen and ceremoniously pours what's left of a fifth of bourbon down the sink. He breaks out another fifth still wrapped with a Christmas ribbon and pours it down the sink. "Your mother tends to overreact and exaggerate from time to time, but I do love her." He doesn't look at her, just keeps pouring. "She doesn't drink, so I won't drink."

"She has never had a problem, " Sally says, and for a brief second Marilyn feels Tom's eyes on her.

"I used to," Marilyn says.

"Yeah, she'd sip a little wine on holidays. Made her feel sick didn't it, honey?" Sid is opening and closing cabinets. He puts on the tea kettle. "Mother likes tea in the late afternoon like the British. As a matter of fact," he continues, still not looking at her, "sometimes we pretend we are British."

She nods and watches him pour out some cheap Scotch he always offers to cheap friends. He keeps the good stuff way up high behind her mother's silver service. "And we've been writing our own little holiday letter, Mother and I, and we're going to tell every single thing that has gone on this past year like Sally and Rusty do. Like I'm going to tell that Mother has a spastic colon and often feels 'sqwitty,' as the British might say, and that I had an abscessed tooth that kept draining into my throat, leaving me no choice but to hock and spit throughout the day. But all that aside, kids, the real reason I can't formally go somewhere to dry out for you right now is (1) I have already booked a hotel over in

Myrtle Beach for our anniversary, and (2) there is nothing about me to dry."

By the end of the night everyone is talking about "one more chance." Sid has easily turned the conversation to Rusty and where he plans to apply to school and to Snow Bunny and her hopes of having a "little Tommy" a year from now. They say things like that they are proud of Sid for his effort but not to be hard on himself if he can't do it on his own. He needs to realize he might have a problem. He needs to be able to say: I have a problem.

"So. Wonder what stirred all that up?" he asks as they watch the children finally drive away. She has yet to make eye contact with him. "I have to say I'm glad to see them leave." He turns now and waits for her to say something.

"I say, 'Adios motherfuckers.'" She cocks her hands this way and that like the rappers do, which makes him laugh. She notices his hand shaking and reaches to hold it in her own. She waits and then she offers to fix him a small drink to calm his nerves.

"I don't have to have it, you know," he says.

"Oh, I know that," she says. "I also know you saved the good stuff."

She mixes a weak one and goes into the living room, where he has turned off all but the small electric candle on the piano.

"Here's to the last drink," he says as she sits down beside him. He breathes a deep sigh that fills the room. He doesn't ask again if she had anything to do with what happened. He never questions her a second time; he never has. And in the middle of the night when she reaches her hand over the cool sheets, she will find him there, and when spring comes and the sticky heat disgusts her with pangs of all the failures in her life, he will be there, and when it is time to get in the car and drive to Myrtle Beach or to see the kids, perhaps even to drive all the way to Minnesota to see their grandchildren, she will get in and close the door to the passenger side without a word. She will turn and look at the house that the two of them worked so hard to maintain and she will note as she always does the perfect green grass of the front yard and how Sid fixed it so that there is not a trace of the mess she made. It is their house. It is their life. She will fasten her seatbelt and not say a word.

ME AND BIG FOOT

IT IS SNOWING, a freak blinding storm that likely will shut things down for days. Thank God. Just last night under a clear winter sky, I had wished for a sign, or at least some kind of divine intervention from the matchmakers of the world—all those well-meaning friends who are far more upset over my single status than I am. They drop by unannounced to offer me comfort and advice and descriptions of various men as if they are hot entrees on a silver platter.

Now I look out my window to see a very large foreign object out there in the blowing snow, a big white rusty truck parked in my side yard. I put on my heavy coat and boots and go out there, circle it a few times. There are no tire tracks leading in or footprints leading out. No license plate or inspection sticker. The front bumper is a two-by-four. A wet note penned on a coffee-stained napkin is under the wiper: *You, cute-looking owner of the little scrappy dog, please don't tow or complain. I need you. Please. I'll be back soon.*

I tug open the heavy iced-over door and climb up into the cab; as soon as I close myself in, all windows glazed in ice, I have the strangest feeling that I've been here before. *I'm not a complainer,* I imagine telling him, *and I hate to be around one.* No key. Only a flashlight and lighter in the glove compartment, a pair of gloves on the dash, the thumbs cut out, palms stiff with resin and dirt. I sit there in the cab, stretch my legs, and feel an odd sense of comfort and warmth.

The truck smells of mildew and woodsmoke. The floorboard is frozen and the seats are damp and frosted, as if he'd driven off road through the swamp. A thick-lipped coffee mug is wedged into the opened ashtray and I run my fingers around the smooth stained rim. Behind the seat there is a big pair of hunting boots covered in red mud and muck. I reach my hands down into those tall sturdy boots and feel the worn thick wool, my body heat slowly absorbed and held there. *I need you.* Had he walked up to my door? *Please.* If so he might have seen me through the sheers, painting my toenails and talking to my friend Sophie, telling her yet again about how I am not going to the Swinging Singles Sing-a-long at her church. She's married—happily, she says—but has made me her project. If he'd waited he might even have heard me there under the sky saying those same words—*Please, I need you*—to the powers of the great beyond.

I DON'T KNOW what it is about a person alone that drives other people crazy. I'm thinking we all heard too many Bible stories coming along—Adam and Eve (that match made in heaven). Or Noah's ark, desperate pairs scurrying onto the love boat, a lesson reinforced by that Irish song we sang to death in grade school about the poor unicorn left crying on a rock because he didn't find somebody he wanted to live with for all eternity.

What's more, people seem to really hate it if you say you're *happy* alone. It makes Sophie so uncomfortable, in fact, that I finally confessed to her that of course I had a dream of my perfect match, but that I also would rather live alone than opt for just any old body who slid up next to me and took root. I talked fast so she wouldn't think I was referring to Kyle, who she married in great haste after only three months. I went on to say that even in my most ideal dream match I would still require a lot of solitary time with limited interruptions from friends and family. I said this very directly since she drops by unannounced all the time and has implied several times that both my house and person need an extreme makeover. She said my bedroom was abominable, that it looked like a cheap motel, and that my clothes were too bad to even give away. Especially the olive-green velvet dress I wore to their Christmas party. Especially since it was cold and I was bare legged. "Well, thank you," I said, hoping to hurry her along, but she was hell-bent on connecting my poor fashion sense to the breakup with Scott months ago even though I have explained many times over that we broke up because I said that I would never marry him and *his* biological clock was ticking. I could not marry him, not now and not ever. We had nothing in common and the fact that I had trouble listening to what he was saying was proof enough that it would be a mistake. And why is that so hard to understand? Why do these people look out there and say: *Hetero and hetero, get on the boat and go. You both need to breathe to stay alive? Great, amazing, now get on the boat and go.* And you say, *I am not the least bit attracted to that person. I hate his politics, the way he chews, the way he finishes my sentence as I'm speaking it.* I can't stand anything worse than a spoiled white boy trying to sound and act like he grew up in the ghetto or a trailer park. That was Scott in a nutshell: privileged gangsta wannabe driving a Hummer and canceling my vote nearly every time. I say, *I cannot live like that. I am better off alone.* And people like Sophie (as if deaf to all else) will say, *But he has such a good job.*

And yes, there is a perfect man in my mind and he has always been there, nameless, faceless, self-sufficient, and therefore free from all societal entrapments, and most important, more loyal than any dog as he remains fiercely rooted in my life. Does he exist? I want to believe that, like all the great abstractions, he might, that with the right angle of the sun or direction of the wind, he could. And now as I sit in this frozen white truck, my warm breath trapped against my mouth by the wool of my scarf, it is like he is here, sitting right there in the passenger seat in his big tall boots, his hands surprisingly smooth for someone so outdoorsy. I close my eyes and he is there; I can smell and taste him, feel his hands pulling me close, and it is like every little pheromone and hormone in my body is waking after a long hibernation, a million little Rip Van Winkles eager to make up for a lot of lost time. I have what is called a major out of body experience. No one could be more surprised than I am.

I GO INSIDE feeling like a new woman. I look in the mirror and I am younger, more alive looking than I have ever been. When Sophie calls, I tell her I'm snowed in with a visiting friend, that no, she's never met him, that yes, I've known him forever. That I am hoping he will stay a few days and I will call later. I go and get his big nasty boots and put them by my front door so when the storm ends it will look like we never left the house. I put on some music, light candles, build a fire. The snow has quieted everything. The power is out. The phone doesn't ring. My whole world pauses.

"WHO IS HE?" Sophie asks after a week, the truck still parked there. She is at my front door in bright yellow ski gear even though little snow remains, and I motion for her to be quiet.

"Still sleeping," I say and point to my closed bedroom door. "He loves my bedroom. I can hardly get him to leave it." She gives me a skeptical look, starts to speak, but catches herself. I whisper over coffee in the kitchen. I tell her all about him. His slow gentle movements and ability to sense my needs and wants before I even speak. I tell her how we're reading things aloud at night—funny columns that make us laugh, political ones that make us mad, poetry that breaks our hearts. How we are working to train little Curly so he will fetch something other than what's in the cat's litter box. It all sounds so wonderful I can hardly believe it myself.

THE TRUCK IS STILL here when the crocuses surface and I like to think this can go on forever. I have gotten so comfortable with it all, the questions, the stories. *We love to just cook and sit by the fire. Take long walks in the woods. We watch lots of old movies. Exercise? Oh, we get plenty.* Wink wink. *Sure, you'll meet him. But he does travel a lot. He works so hard and plays hard, too.*

Sophie says everyone has noticed how I often look glassy-eyed and rumpled like someone just rolled from the bed, that one day she would have sworn I had a hickey, which really did shock her. I laughed and blushed for real because sometimes—before going to the store or anyplace I might see people—I do pinch my neck and roll around and rub against the indoor/outdoor carpet on my stairs. I have to confess I kind of like the way it feels there on all fours, so primal and earthy, like an animal following a scent. Sometimes I start laughing and can't stop. The cat thinks I'm making fun of him and swishes off into another room but Curly sees my position as an open invitation to join in with some dog-like behavior and I just thank god he's a ten-pound dust ball and not the 110-pound Rottweiler I once tended at a shelter.

Word is out that my man is kind of antisocial. The talkers tell how he always has been a little bit of a loner, and with good reason. He is wanted everywhere he goes. His advice, his expertise, his big strong body and intellect and winning ways. Besides, he's an archaeologist out there digging around in the forests and riverbanks while they are sleeping. "He's nocturnal," I say. "And there are certainly worse things."

FULL SPRING AND I never tire of closing my eyes and seeing him there. He is the best man I've ever known. He never mentions if my legs are prickly or toenail polish chipped or if I look plumper or my breath smells of baked Brie or garlic. He doesn't care that I don't have much money and am not ready to have a kid, that I eat snacks in bed and keep the house cold year round so that I can wear layers and pile up quilts and blankets. He doesn't care that my bedroom looks like the Days Inn. In fact, because we are so much alike, he *likes* it. And he *loves* that green fringed dress of mine, thinks it's the sexiest thing I own. He sometimes likes for me to wear it while I clean his big dirty boots and he washes the dishes and changes the sheets. He likes four-hundred-count sheets, which is a little contradiction about him that I just adore. We would rather have soft sheets than sexy shoes. And, of course, because he is that way, it makes me want to please him even more, to be as desirable as I can be. And there is the difference: desire.

My man was created in my image and then roughed up in a way I have always found very attractive. He *is* me only big and hairy and forceful in every way. He's the man I'd want to be. At night when I get there under my warm quilts piled high like a cave, I am waiting for him to return. The anticipation of his arrival is all I need—I can't wait for him to grab my hips and spoon up close to my backside or for the way I might wake and turn in his direction, nuzzling in like a heat-seeking missile to the comfort I've come to depend on, his desiring hands there in the darkness nothing more than extensions of my own.

By April, no one believes that anyone can be so perfect, so I give him seasonal allergies and a big white car-wreck scar on his clavicle. I give him a childhood just unhappy enough to develop his artistic sensitivity and compassion. I give him a sweet early heartache that keeps him romantic and longing to recreate a pure and perfect love. Though health conscious and in really great shape, he does love the occasional smoke, good bourbon, and pork any way he can get it.

"You are a phenomenon of the first degree," I whisper to him as

I fall asleep. I say, "You are a giant of a man, a magical and mythical wonder." I call him Sass and Skookum, Yeti, Momo, Yowie. He just calls me "baby"or "sweetheart," which out of his mouth is like nothing I've ever heard. I tell him how he will never want to wander too far from our own secret cave—there away from all the others. I tell him I will slide my way over coarse rock and stone, wade the icy riverbed through the deepest darkest forest to find him, that I am forever marked by his scent.

FRIENDS HAVE BEGUN to see him and report to one another. It's a competition like *Where's Waldo?* or an Elvis sighting. He's a local legend by now. He's been seen several times on the riverbank, a man nearly seven feet tall with a stringer of enough fish to feed the whole county. "They were delicious, too," I say. "He used a recipe he made up himself that was once published in *Gourmet* magazine."

One person saw him at Food City with two cases of wine and a huge whole ham hoisted up on one shoulder. He talked to her and told her that the two of us would be having a big party one of these days soon, probably after his next expedition to the Arctic. Another saw him at Dainty Pat's Pastries buying little fruit tarts. He held the door open for that mean elderly man no one in town likes and then shared a laugh with her; she said he asked her for coffee so he'd get to know some of my friends better, but she just didn't have time. "He's sexy, all right," she said to me, and it made me feel good but also really mad. I wanted to tell her to find her own man.

When I get tired of all the sightings, I send him on a big dig for a month and then I tell them all about our last night together and the bracelet (ordered late one night on the Internet) he gave me so I would know with its weight that he is always thinking of me. It's a silver cuff that wraps smooth and cold against my skin. People (including Sophie) think I am so lucky in love they are contemplating a change in wardrobe and bedroom furniture. *Of course you're fine alone,* they say now. *You're waiting for him.*

But today I come home from the store, my bag filled with wine and roses and those big sea scallops he loves to sauté in butter, and the truck is gone. There is a note on my door penned in a hasty scrawl. *Thanks for not calling the cops.* My heart sinks as if I have been abandoned, as if I will never see him again, and then I remember that of course he'll be back. What's more, he has left his boots there by my front door, clean, ready, and waiting for his return.